THE DOUBLE RUN

Prisoner at the Bar
To Protect the Guilty
Bent Copper
A Man Will Be Kidnapped Tomorrow

Jeffrey Ashford

THE DOUBLE RUN

WALKER AND COMPANY • NEW YORK

First published in the United States of America
in 1973 by the Walker Publishing Company, Inc.

ISBN: 0-8027-5288-8

Library of Congress Catalog Card Number: 73-83193

Printed in the United States of America

10 9 8 7 6 5 4 3 2 1

1

The SEAT was too long and its steering too poor for the more acute hairpins and three times Hilary Ryan had to take them in two locks. It was beautiful, remote country, in the foothills of the Majorcan Sierra de Alfabia, and the road looped like a snake in torment as it wound its way up and down over tree-covered hills where only the very occasional farmhouse showed that men did live and work some of the land.

Algendar was on the side of a hill whose rocky top towered over the village and seemed sullenly to threaten it. There was a huddle of houses, stepped to match the contours on either side of the road, and a rough square with a large well in the centre. He drove past children playing with a ball and they stared at the car with an interest that clearly showed how few strange cars went through, then he was clear of the village. The road climbed steeply to the crest of the hill, turned sharply round an outcrop of grey rock which was streaked with blue, plunged down into a pine-covered valley. Isolation once more became complete.

Three kilometres, the man had said. He watched the odometer so carefully that after three-quarters of a kilometre he almost ran into a donkey cart. The driver, old, weather-beaten, stubble-chinned, bare to the waist with skin the colour of mahogany, seemed unperturbed by the encounter and hardly bothered to look at the SEAT: nine parts asleep, thought Ryan.

As the three kilometres clicked up, he saw the ruin of the house on the left, fifty feet above the road and perched on the spur of bare rock. It was a magnificent site for anyone who wanted total isolation free of any amenity.

The right-hand bend, just negotiable in one lock, was two hundred metres on and immediately beyond was hard-packed bare earth by the side of the road which provided a rough lay-by. He parked here and climbed out of the car. A familiar tension, together with the heat, brought out the sweat and he mopped his face and neck with a handkerchief.

The area was very heavily wooded, mainly with pines, and the boughs of trees almost met overhead, so that the road became a shimmering battleground between harsh sunlight and sharp shadows.

He became conscious of the silence, undisturbed except by the constant chorus of cicadas, when there was the brief tinkling of a bell. The sound was repeated, though further away, and from the other side of the road and he identified it as coming from bells attached to the necks of either sheep or goats which must be freely grazing the very bare pasture under the trees.

Time passed and the unusual peace soothed him until he'd almost forgotten his purpose for being there, then he heard the whine of a car which was being driven fast, despite the nature of the road. There was tyre squeal as another SEAT came round the right-hand bend. It parked immediately in front of his car. A tall man, an inch more than Ryan's six feet, stepped out. He had a lop-sided face in which it seemed as if the right half had sunk, his hair was very black and was so plastered down with hair grease it sparkled when the sunlight touched it, and his eyes held the calculating gaze of a man who always knew how to make something for himself. 'Good afternoon,' he said, his voice heavily accented yet perfectly understandable.

The man's face seemed to be familiar and Ryan tried to remember if and where he'd seen it before. 'Good morning,' he answered, thus identifying himself.

The man stared at him with the same inquisitive curiosity, then his expression suddenly changed to one of fear and he reached under his coat and pulled out a small dagger.

Ryan stared at the knife in an amazement that abruptly changed to a stomach-churning terror and he only avoided the first thrust by instinctive movement, his mind not yet having caught up with events. He turned and began to run, tripped over a large stone, and fell to his knees. Instead of coming to his feet, he found the sense to drop to the ground and roll over.

The dagger spitted the air where he'd been. They ran. At first, Ryan had a lead of four or five feet as he raced between the trees, his breath already beginning to come with difficulty, but then the ground sloped upwards more steeply and he missed a foothold and half fell, his right foot sending a scattering of small stones downwards.

It was absurd, he thought wildly, as he lunged to

7

the left—the other man was obviously frightened, yet was desperately trying to murder him. 'Look . . .' he croaked. The dagger ripped through his trousers and he felt the icy cool of the blade as it crossed his flesh: had it been edged, he would have been cut.

He lashed out with his right foot and had the luck to catch the other in the crutch. There was a grunted cry of pain and the dagger was dropped. He grabbed it and drove it home into the man's stomach. It pierced the clothes and slid in easily for a couple of inches, met some resistance, but then, as the other surged forward, slid in another two inches.

The man's immediate expression was one of confused surprise. He held his balance, looked at Ryan, and down at the hilt of the dagger as it stuck out of his fawn-coloured linen trousers. Around the point of entry there was as yet only a faint seepage of discoloured blood and the trousers were almost unstained. Moving slowly, he took hold of the handle of the knife to pluck it out but as he began to pull he gave a thin, warbling scream of pain. Mouth open, he collapsed on to his knees, overbalanced and fell flat. The knife was driven further in and twisted sideways. He screamed again, and this time it sounded as if his mouth was half filled with liquid, gave one convulsive jerk, and lay still.

2

The November rain, blown by a near-gale-force easterly wind, lashed the sitting-room windows of Thorndale House.

Anderson jerked his thumb. 'It sounds a right old night for tramps and lovers!' He fanned out his cards. 'I'll tell you what: I'll make it easy for you. Only ten to see me.'

'I'm away,' replied Peter Comyns, brushing his moustache. One of the least adventurous of poker players, he seldom found the courage to bluff or, when fairly sure another player was bluffing, to call it.

'Me too.' Polly Comyns threw in her cards. 'I can't lose any more housekeeping—if Pete has to eat cold meat more than once a week he gets like a bear with sore you-know-what.' She chuckled and was not in the least perturbed when her husband glared quickly at her to express dislike of her typically suggestive coarseness. She was a plump woman and, as she so often cheerfully said, careless of the fact: life was for enjoying and one of her enjoyments was eating.

Nina Ryan had thrown in her hand without bothering to buy cards. She wasn't really fond of poker, but played it to make up the numbers.

Ryan hesitated. He had three fours. Anderson had bought three cards and could easily have only the pair he started with, yet he was a lucky player who often confounded the odds.

'Four aces beats my pair of deuces,' said Anderson and laughed loudly. He did everything loudly. When he'd been assembled, the Almighty had forgotten the soft pedal.

Did Anderson's boisterous confidence really signify what his hand was like? Ryan looked at his three fours again. They were just too low to risk. He threw in.

'Well I'm damned! No one ready to have a look at my busted flush?'

Ryan picked up the cards and managed to refrain from checking what Anderson's hand had really been —something he'd have dearly liked to know. He stood up. 'Who's having one for the road?'

'I'll take a whisky off you,' said Anderson immediately. 'Just so long as old Pete doesn't whip out a breathalyser and demand a puff before we go. What about it, eh, Pete?' He grinned cockily at Comyns, who ignored him.

Anderson never missed a chance of riling Comyns, thought Ryan, as he crossed to the cocktail cabinet. It was often amusing to listen to: the matador goading the heavy thundering bull who never quite managed to catch him. Ryan poured out a strong whisky and handed the glass to Anderson, asked Comyns what he wanted and was told nothing in a rather puritanical tone of voice, and gave himself another gin and tonic.

Conversation was desultory and Polly yawned, not bothering to conceal the fact. 'I'm ready for bed.'

It was too easy an opportunity for Anderson to miss. 'So why don't you and I go, then?'

'You've got a dirty mind, Ted.'

'It's that which keeps me young and healthy.'

10

Comyns said: 'We must go: it's late.' He was never amused by Anderson's repartee, but his wife so often joined in enthusiastically that he didn't openly object.

Anderson and Ryan finished their drinks. Polly, as always, offered to help clear up, but Nina thanked her and said it wasn't necessary. They moved into the rectangular hall.

Comyns helped Polly into her green coat, bought a year ago at Marks and Spencer, and Anderson pulled on his new short overcoat bought at Sands and Dors a week ago for ninety-five pounds—as he had twice told them on arrival.

The new overcoat suited Anderson, thought Ryan reluctantly. For a man with such general poor taste it was extraordinary how Anderson managed to choose clothes which made him look discreetly smart. Or maybe one of his women provided the service.

Polly said goodbye and kissed each of them on the cheek. Her husband waited with growing impatience, opened the front door, and shooed her out as she, with humorous indignation, told him there was all the time in the world, as it was Sunday tomorrow and a late lie-in.

'Well, as Keats used to say, "Weary with toil, I haste me to my bed",' said Anderson—a quotation that came easily to his lips. He slapped Ryan on the back.

It was typical of the other to get his poets wrong, thought Ryan. But then Anderson wasn't really concerned about anything but making money.

The rain had eased off, but the wind was as strong. The Comyns reached their car, a battered Hillman, hurriedly climbed in and drove off immediately. Anderson stepped into his new V12 Jaguar, switched on and started the engine and then blipped it several times as if he had to make certain the plugs didn't wet up. Playing at being a racing driver, thought Ryan sarcastically. He looked across at the unlit upstairs windows of the house opposite: if the Smiths were woken up by the noise they'd certainly say their piece. Finally, Anderson drove away with acceleration fierce enough to spin the wheels and half-slew the car across the road.

Ryan yawned as he shut and bolted the front door. 'Let's skip the clearing up until the morning and just have a last night-cap instead?'

'I'd rather do it now,' Nina replied. 'And I don't think I want any more to drink.'

He wondered, as he followed her into the sitting-room, whether she'd ever overcome the influence of her mother who'd dinned it into her that no well-brought-up person could ever leave a muddle in the house overnight.

They carried the dirty plates and glasses into the very well-equipped kitchen and stacked them in the washing-up machine. 'I think Edward's getting worse,' she said. 'He wasn't really in the house before he told us for the first time how much that coat of his had cost.'

'He had to be certain we noticed it.'

She smiled. 'You don't seriously think anyone could miss it? A coat likes that makes a man really stand out.'

'Does it? Then maybe I ought to buy myself one?'

'Will you?' she said immediately, accepting his words as having been spoken seriously. 'Something like that would go so beautifully with you'

He clipped shut the door of the washir

'If I buy so much as a packet of buttons '
lowered the overdraft, the bank manager will
seizure.'

'Why worry about him? Darling, do treat yourself.'

He shook his head. Even now, after ten years of
marriage, she could still surprise him by her un-
realistic approach to money, her refusal to understand there was not an unlimited supply of it. Not
that he begrudged her the pleasure she got from
spending it.

'How did you end up tonight, darling?' she asked,
changing the subject abruptly.

'I think I'm about a pound up.'

'Well, I lost a pound, so that leaves us all square.
I suppose Edward must have won again because both
Polly and Pete said they'd lost.'

'Money always runs after money.'

'I wonder just how much he does make in a year
from his work?'

'One thing's for sure, it's a hell of a lot more than
I do. You ought to marry him and then you could
have that little mink coat you took a shine to in Rob-
sons.'

'Thank you for nothing.'

'Merely a suggestion.' He grinned.

'It's fun having him here and visiting his place—
except when he gets too *nouveau riche*—but to be
married to him . . . Now there is a fate worse than
death!'

'Why?' he asked curiously.

'Because there's something about him a little . . .

13

Slimy?' She shook her head. 'No, that's not it. Calculating. Everything's checked to see what's in it for him. The only reason he'd marry is if he could find a woman who'd bring him more than she cost.'

'From all accounts, he doesn't actually need to get married.'

'Judging by the blonde I saw him with the other day, that's true if it's only sex he's after.'

'I doubt he was interested in her capabilities as a cook.'

They went upstairs. After returning from the bathroom, she began to undress. 'Don't forget we're taking Jack and some pal of his down to the docks at Meeriton tomorrow afternoon.'

'I hadn't. D'you know what it's all in aid of?'

'Only to see the boats. He still seems very keen on going to sea when he's old enough.'

He watched her unbuckle her brassière. She had a thickish body, not yet really plump but not far from it and this was a surer guide to her age than her face, which was round, unlined, pleasantly featured, and able to absorb the years without comment. He crossed to her side, kissed her, and began to fondle her. After a while, she gently edged him away and said she was sorry, but she was really too tired. She was often tired.

He finished undressing and climbed into the left-hand side of the very large double bed. When they'd been newly married, he remembered nostalgically, her passion had almost matched his, so that there had been some very lively scenes indeed, but somehow over the intervening years she'd come to respond less and less. It was a pity, but the experience of friends suggested that it was virtually inevitable:

14

women, they said sadly, found their pleasures in other ways.

She read for only a few minutes, then switched off her light, turned and kissed him good night. He would have read on, not feeling tired, but switched off his light so as not to keep her awake.

He wondered if Ted Anderson really was so wealthy that he didn't have to spent most of his life making one penny do the work of two? Broadly speaking, money was the only worry Nina and he had. They spent every penny he made, and more. Thorndale House was in an expensive suburb of Rushton, but as Nina had said when they'd considered buying it, in a period of inflation a house was almost the only solid investment available: although an 'expensive' investment because of the sizable mortgage they'd had to take out. Nina liked to entertain a lot and why not? But entertaining cost money, especially when there was the usual friendly rivalry to see who could offer the most lavish hospitality.

He heard her breathe deeply as she always did when on the point of falling asleep. Her parents had always been wealthy so that she believed the standard of living to which she was accustomed was virtually a God-given right. His parents had never been wealthy and because his father had been a very active Mason, a leading member of the local golf club, past president of the local cricket club, a man who entertained as if his bank account were bottomless—not from any inferiority complex, but because that was what he liked doing—his mother had sometimes been at her wits' end to pay the housekeeping bills. From his mother he must surely have inherited

15

his inherent cautiousness, his due sense of con-
formity, from his father the occasional dreams of the
delights of irresponsibility: normally, there was
little doubt in his mind that a man was properly employed in a job that, above all, offered security, but
just occasionally he dreamt of bursting free and finding out what life was like beyond.

He turned over and by accident his right hand
touched her. He ran his hand lightly over her but-
tock. Looked at sanely, their marriage had been a
level, happy, pleasant one, virtually unstrained by
rows: only in the wilder parts of his mind did he
query the value of the evenness of it, the lack of peaks
of either misery or exaltation.

She moved slightly as if in response to his caress.
Then she almost snored and he knew she was in
reality asleep. He removed his hand before he reached
the stage—imaginary, as he well knew—where he'd
wake her up and demand passionate relief.

He'd been lucky in life. The job at Llanarch
Motors had been vacant just when he was ready to
leave his previous firm. Well paid, it would provide
a very useful and important stepping stone to a
higher position, preferably in the same firm.

Llanarch Motors made lousy cars, he thought, as
the waves of sleep began to surge through his mind.
But then old man Llanarch had lived by the creed
that it was stupid to build a product in any degree
better than to the minimum standard demanded by
an unthinking public—a creed that had turned him
into a millionaire and brought him a knighthood a
couple of years before he died.

3

Situated roughly between Rushton, once a pleasant market town but now ruined by overspill housing and industrialisation, and the county town of Abston Cross was the sprawling factory complex of Llanarch Motors. Sir Gwilym Llanarch had always indignantly denied the suggestion that his factories despoiled the countryside, yet, as a local councillor had once pointed out, it did seem as if he had searched far and wide for the most naturally beautiful area that he could ruin. When the original factory had been built, no one had really bothered about the destruction of beauty: only when more and more buildings sprawled out to engulf acres of lush green fields, ancient copses of oaks, elms, ashes, the only known habitat of a unique member of the genus of orchid Cypripedium, and newt-filled ponds, did the conservationists complain, Sir Gwilyn was very annoyed by such ingratitude—since when did beauty bear any real value? When he died, his marble mausoleum was generally agreed to be every bit as ugly as his factories.

Llanarch cars had, during Sir Gwilym's lifetime, always been as badly designed and finished as any British car, which was something of a distinction. After his death there had followed a period of re-adjustment, reorganisation, and rationalisation, and at the end of this upheaval the new management produced a range of cars that were conservative

17

and unimaginative but adequate and which would, if very carefully looked after, last almost as long as the cheaper of the imports.

Ryan drove his Antares—Llanarch models were now named after the more pronounceable stars instead of totally unpronounceable Welsh mountains—up to the main gates of the administrative building and the nearer security guard waved him on. An Altair, just off the assembly line, whipped past at over fifty as the driver ignored both the fifteen m.p.h. factory speed limit and the forty-five running-in limit, on its way to the nearest parking lot. Ryan drew into the first space reserved for the P.R.O. department: the higher one's job grading, the nearer the main doors one was allowed to park.

The building was eleven floors high and ugly in an aggressive manner. From the roof, one could see green tree-clad hills to the north and, if the wind took the factory's polluting smoke clear, the glint of the sea to the south. Press and publicity were on the fifth floor, along with the legal adviser and overflow accounts.

He went into his room. Davies was already working at his desk, which was to be expected. Davies was always a few minutes early because there wasn't anything he wouldn't do to create a good impression.

' 'Morning,' said Ryan. 'What's the news? Another two thousand Llanarch cars rusted away in the night?'

Davies nervously looked towards the door. He disliked blasphemy.

Ryan sat down and lit a cigarette and was amused by the look Davies gave him. Inside the other's

18

bulky body there was a mouse of a man trying desperately to stay where he was.

The intercom unit buzzed and Ryan flicked down a switch. 'Ryan here.'

There was the characteristic quick cough. 'Would you please come along to my office right away.'

'I'm on my way.' Ryan stood up and stubbed out his cigarette. 'What's got old Chapel croaking this early in the morning?'

Davies shook his head.

Ryan left and went along to the large and well-furnished office of Chapel, director of press, public relations, and advertising. Chapel was a small, fussy, didactic man in his late middle-age who had been with the firm for thirty-five years and survived all the reorganisations because he was very good at the one thing which really mattered, agreeing with the decisions of the directors. He wore horn-rimmed glasses and his old school tie and there was always a handkerchief in the breast pocket of his coat.

When Ryan entered, Chapel cleared his throat and stared at a point a few inches to the right of Ryan's head. 'Do you know why I've called you in here?' he asked at last.

'No, I don't.' Ryan looked round for a chair and saw that the two usually in front of the desk had been carefully placed against a wall.

'It's on account of the photograph which appeared in *L'Auto* in July.'

'That! Are people still worried about that?' A very clear photograph of the new 2·5 luxury Aldebaren had appeared in the French magazine a month before official press release. This happened to all manufacturers. Someone saw a prototype or one of the pre-production models out on the roads, only thinly disguised, photographed it, and then made what he could out of the photograph . . . which usually was very little, or nothing.

'The chairman was very perturbed,' said Chapel.

'So we heard at the time.'

'So perturbed that he ordered an investigation into how the photograph came to be published.' Chapel took off his spectacles and cleaned the lenses with a tissue he took from a drawer. He waited for some comment, but when none came he added: 'A private detective was employed to uncover the truth.'

'That's using a sledgehammer to crack a nut, isn't it?'

'Not in the opinion of the board.' Chapel replaced the spectacles. He fidgeted with the handkerchief in his breast pocket, then blurted out: 'It was you who sent the photo to the magazine.'

'I did what?' Ryan smiled. 'You surely can't really believe that?'

'We know it was you.'

Ryan ceased to be amused. 'Then you don't know anything. What in the hell . . .?'

'We have the proof.'

Ryan stared at Chapel, whose face was frozen in and expression of determined antagonism. 'What proof?'

Chapel pressed down a switch on the intercom. 'Ask Mr. Jones to come in, please.' He sat back in the chair and stared fixedly through the window.

'Look, God knows what's been going on,' said Ryan, 'but let's get the records dead straight. I don't know a damn thing about that photograph. In any case, the whole matter's so trivial . . .'

'The board does not agree.'

'It wouldn't. That would be far too sensible an attitude to take.'

There was a knock on the door and Jones entered. He was tall and thin, with a long, lean head that seemed out of proportion with his body. His expression was one of resigned pessimism, as if he always expected the worst and was seldom disappointed. His clothes had the hangdog look of cheap ready-to-wears which had had a hard life.

'This is Ryan,' said Chapel.

Ryan nodded curtly in answer to the other's rushed greeting. He was struck by the unusual redness of Jones's face and ears and the contrast between this and the whiteness of his nearly bald head.

'Will you please go over the facts, Mr. Jones.'

Jones had a high, almost squeaky voice, and he tended to lisp his Rs. He spoke tonelessly, as if giving evidence in the witness-box. 'I was detailed to find out how a photograph of the new model was sent to a French magazine a month before the press release. I carried out all normal enquiries, both here and in France, and in the course of these discovered certain facts.' He took a small notebook from his pocket and opened it. 'The French office gave me the photo and the letter which had accompanied it. The letter, typed and unsigned, had a comprehensive and accurate list of the specifications of the new model, called the Alde . . . Aldebaren . . .' He stumbled a little over the pronounciation. 'I discovered that all pre-release photos of new models were numbered as a security measure. From the number on the photo I was able to ascertain that it had originally been issued to you, three weeks prior to the day it was received in Paris.'

'To me?' said Ryan, now a shade uneasy.

'That is correct.'

'Hell, man! D'you think I'm such a fool I'd send this photo on knowing it could be traced back to me?'

'The sender probably imagined no proper investigation would ever be carried out.'

'But even so, no one in his right senses would do that.'

'The figures had been inked out so that the sender must have believed it was unreadable. I had a forensic laboratory carry out tests and because a different ink had been used to the original one, infra-red light with the Westland technique showed up the number.'

Ryan suddenly and belatedly realised that though Jones might look ill at ease and seedy, he was very thorough and no fool . . . The number said this photograph must have come from his room . . . Had he not filed it but left it lying around in the usual clutter on the desk? . . . Just because it had been one of the set issued to him . . . 'All right, so it was originally mine. Obviously, someone came into my office and swiped it.'

Jones said, his voice monotonously even in tone: 'I took a sample or typewriting from the typewriter on you desk and this was compared with the letter. They match and it's quite certain the letter was written on your machine.'

Ryan's sense of unease merged into one of anger. 'So that merely proves that the person who pinched the photo also used my typewriter.'

Jones made no comment.

'Why should I have sent it?'

'I can't tell you because I don't know.'

'But I do.' said Chapel, speaking loudly. He was sitting very upright in his chair.

Ryan turned. 'All right. Tell.'

'It was a stupid, juvenile, thumb-to-nose tilt at authority.'

'What the hell are you talking about?'

'Shortly before the letters and photos were sent to France. I had occasion to reprimand you severely.'

At first Ryan couldn't remember the trouble, then it came back to him. Ever the pedant, Chapel had discovered that incorrect statistics had been sent out in the Flemish translation of the weekly newsletter. The statistics were of little significance and the sales of Llanarchs to Belgium were very small, so that the mistake, which in any case had been the translator's fault, was very minor indeed, but Chapel had tried to make out it was of major importance. Ryan had treated his expressed concern with an amused contempt he'd made little effort to hide: Chapel had huffed and puffed and read the riot act. 'You really think I worried about that?' asked Ryan, and then realised a man of Chapel's character would take further offence at having his reprimand treated so obviously cavalierly.

That Chapel did take further offence was evidenced by the sudden tightening set of his lips. 'The board of directors,' he said, 'have discussed the matter at very great length and in full detail and we are all greatly perturbed by it.'

The royal 'We', thought Ryan: Chapel never missed an opportunity to remind his listeners that he was on the board.

23

'It is not the kind of spirit we try to foster in this firm.'

Ryan could not resist the quick answer. 'But you've obviously succeeded in doing so.'

Chapel tapped on the desk. 'In view of all the circumstances, and I repeat all, we have regretfully decided to ask you for your resignation.' He lingered over the word 'regretfully'.

'You what?' Ryan's voice rose. 'You want my resignation over the publication of some piffling photo which was nothing to do with me? You can whistle! I'm not going to be anybody's scapegoat.'

Chapel took off his glasses and polished them again. It was a mannerism he employed to cover up any one of several emotions. He spoke to Jones without looking at him. 'Thank you, Mr. Jones. You'll send me your written report as soon as possible, won't you?'

Jones said goodbye.

Ryan leaned forward and thumped the desk. 'I'm not resigning.'

Chapel replaced his glasses and stared beyond Ryan. 'I am authorised by the board to say that if you resign the reason for your resignation will not be made public and we will give you perfectly reasonable references and a small *ex-gratia* payment. On the other hand, if you see fit to refuse this generous offer ...'

'This what?' demanded Ryan, with furious sarcasm.

Chapel continued speaking as if there had been no interruption. 'The company will have no alternative but to dismiss you from its employment. Should you then be so ill-advised as to challenge their

action, all the evidence against you will be adduced.'
He coughed his dry cough. 'In the latter circumstances, of course, you would undoubtedly not find it easy to secure another responsible position.'

.   .   .   .   .

Ryan stepped out of the administrative building and the cold east wind dug fingers of ice into him. Hastily he pulled on his overcoat. Over the hills, a vast grey cloud was dropping a curtain of freezing rain.

As he stood on the top step, five Altairs went past on their way to a park: on the left-hand bend their tyres squealed as their drivers enjoyed an impromptu dice. They could break the rules and get away with it, he thought bitterly, because if they went on strike the factory choked to a halt—but when he was wrongly suspected of having broken a rule . . .

He began to walk towards his car. Presumably the chairman had set the whole thing in motion, but once it seemed Hilary Ryan might be involved Chapel must have done everything in his power to keep it going at full blast. Chapel was methodically efficient, but he was uneasy in his personal relations with others and he lacked any spark of inspiration: the director of press, public relations, and advertising needed to be able to get on with anyone and at times to be inspired. In the years that Ryan had worked at Llanarch Motors, Chapel had come to hate him because he knew who of the two could do his job the better. Indeed, each of them in his own manner had wondered when Ryan would be made director of the department. So now Chapel had seized his

chance to get rid of the opposition with the ruthless-
ness of the frightened coward.

Ryan was so immersed in his own bitter
thoughts that he almost bumped into Jones as the
latter was stepping into an old and very tatty Vauxhall.

Ryan spoke harshly. 'I didn't send that photo.'

Jones stepped back and stared at him.

'D'you hear—I didn't send it.'

'I've at no stage said you did.' Jones was uneasy,
but not afraid, in face of such open hostility.

'You told that bloody old fool . . .'

'Just the facts. I didn't draw a single conclusion.'

The first few heavy spots of rain spattered down.

'I'll fight them,' said Ryan.

Jones fiddled with the lobe of his right ear. 'Is that
wise?' he finally asked.

'If I didn't send the stuff no one's going to make out
I did.'

'You don't think . . . ? Well, I mean, wouldn't it
be better to accept their offer?'

'And virtually admit guilt? When I'm completely
innocent?'

'It's what other people think in a case like this, not
what the truth is.'

'You're a great detective if you can talk like that.'

'I've seen what can happen.' Jones spoke dis-
piritedly.

'I've a damn sight more faith than you in justice.'

Jones shrugged his shoulders. 'I'd place my trust
in expediency. I've known people hurt bad through
fighting for their rights.' He suddenly spoke urgently.
'Swallow your pride, Mr. Ryan, and take the references, but make certain they're good.' He sounded

26

really concerned about persuading Ryan to do the most sensible thing—as if he had doubts about the decision the company had taken and wanted to salve his conscience over his part.

'I'm not taking the coward's way out.'

Jones's expression became more pessimistic. 'It's your decision.' He got into the car, then spoke again before slamming the door shut. 'My job takes me round a bit. It's not all that easy these days getting another good job when one's been made redundant at your sort of age, so it pays to try to make things as easy as possible for oneself.'

The car drove off. Ryan reluctantly, but inevitable, began to wonder if Jones could be right and there were times when a man was a fool to fight for truth and justice?

4

Nina sat on the settee—an expensive reproduction of an ornate William Kent piece she had insisted on buying the previous year even though he'd protested they couldn't afford it—and fidgeted with the sock she was darning. 'But with all you've said, Hilary, you can't fight them.'

He stood with his back to the fireplace, on the mantelpiece of which were a 365-day clock, two cups

27

Jack had won at school sports at the end of the summer term, and a framed photograph of the three of them taken two years before at Rimini.

'The private detective has to be right,' she said.
'Does he?'

'Stop being so stubborn . . .'

'Shouldn't one be stubborn when fighting for truth?' He tried to sound as if he'd no doubts at all.

Her voice sharpened. 'You're being so . . .' She stopped.

He could guess she had been going to call him pompous. She was really scared. She saw him fighting the company, losing, being bankrupted, thrown into a debtor's prison . . . She was brave about so many things which seemed to frighten most women, yet the merest hint of financial disaster unnerved her.

Her voice became pleading. 'I know how you feel about all those sort of things, but you've got to be realistic.'

Did she really understand how he felt about justice? Most of his beliefs had been inculcated in him by his father who'd read for the Bar but never qualified and who in many ways had been an idealist. He'd been brought up to believe absolutely in English justice—Continental law, his father had told him in all seriousness, couldn't be any good because it didn't boast a Magna Carta. Democracy, English style of course, was a precious thing which each man should be ready to fight for. He still thought like that, though he'd never put his feelings too freely into words, knowing that in an age of general belittlement they'd make him sound very square and fairly ridiculous.

When he made no comment, she spoke again. 'Sup-

28

pose you tried to fight them—what would it cost?'

He shrugged his shoulders.

'You don't worry about that end of things, do you?'

'But I didn't send the photo.'

'Of course you didn't.' She struggled to find the right words to express herself. 'But they believe you did. And they're so much bigger than you. You can't really fight anyone that big. And if you don't fight them, they've promised you good references and some sort of payment. You'll get another job without any trouble. Please, Hilary, don't fight them so we lose everything. I'm . . . I'm scared.'

Her large brown eyes, so quick to reflect her emotions, filled with tears. He went across and sat down by her side and put his arm round her shoulder, stroked her neck with his thumb. It was difficult to be a knight in shining armour, fighting for justice without regard to the cost, when one's wife was so scared. Martyrdom could be an expensive luxury: compromise could be the means of survival.

She took hold of his left hand. 'It would be so terrible if anything happened to us with this house and everything.'

He looked round the sitting-room. The curtains and the carpet were of luxury quality—as witness their bank overdraft. The cocktail cabinet was very well stocked with bottles. In the bow-fronted cabinet, bought from the antique shop run by a couple of queers just round the corner, was her growing collection of silver decanter labels. On the south wall were two prints of Old Rushton which had cost twenty pounds each. On the low coffee table in natural pine were two glossy, expensive illustrated books. The rented colour TV stood in the far corner. No one could mistake the degree of quiet luxury, a luxury Nina seemed to need.

He finished his drink. It seemed absurd that he could now seriously doubt the wisdom of fighting for the truth and proving his honesty, yet, remembering the evidence, Chapel's vindictiveness, and the promise to make his going easy if he went voluntarily, but bloody uncomfortable if he didn't. . . .

.   .   .   .   .

Comyns won a fair-sized king pot with three tens. He looked at his watch and said it was time to eat and Polly left the dining-room to go to the kitchen to fetch the sandwiches she had prepared earlier.

Anderson finished his whisky and put the glass down on the table with a slight thump. Comyns ignored the hint, but it was impossible to tell whether this was deliberate or because he hadn't recognised it for what it was. It seldom was possible to judge his thoughts: he was a man who seemed to keep all his emotions in cold storage. Polly had once giggled and told Nina that underneath that austere exterior there beat a truly emotional heart, but this was after several drinks at Anderson's flat.

Comyns collected up the cards and riffled them into a pack with slow and deliberate movements. He seldom hurried over anything, but no one who knew him at all well ever made the mistake of believing that his methodical ways meant he was really a bit dim. The villains of Rushton named him a right sharp bastard.

Anderson took a pigskin cigar case from his breast pocket and offered it round. 'So, how's the world with everyone today? Selling thousands of cars and catching thousands of criminals?'

Ryan twisted the newly lit cigar round in his fingers. 'As a matter of fact, I've just quit the job.' He tried to sound casual.

'Well, I'll be kicked where it makes a man sing contralto! Good for you, Hilary boy. As I've always said, you're far too bright to be stuck in some stinking factory office, working for a bunch of morons. So what are you going to do? Start up a P.R. firm of your own and pocket a fortune?'

'I haven't sat back and decided yet.'

'That's the right attitude. Take your time and make certain you do what's best for number one. Now don't forget, if there's any advice or any help I can give, just come running. I know a few blokes who could be useful and they owe me a favour, or two.' He winked. He managed to suggest that they owed him whole shiploads.

Comyns looked at Ryan with his pale blue eyes that were the first thing most people noticed about him. 'I thought you were hoping to take over the whole department?'

Ryan smiled as he tried to hide his annoyance at so direct a question. 'I decided it was no good waiting until I'm grey-haired. Chapel seems to have become a fixture.'

'That's the right attitude!' said Anderson. 'Nothing venture, nothing gain, as Moses said when he started off across the Red Sea. But you Pete, you're too much of a stick-in-the-mud to understand.'

Unperturbed by the boisterously expressed

criticism, Comyns left the table and opened a bottle of Spanish wine. He poured out five glassfuls which he passed round the table. 'It's not a time I'd choose to go job-hunting, with all the redundancies that are going on—but, of course, if you're starting up on your own, that's different.'

Polly returned to the dining-room with a large plate of sandwiches on a slightly chipped wooden tray. Anderson raised his glass. 'To the cook, God bless her!' He drank. 'This is nice wine, Pete.'

Why did Anderson have to lie so patently and thoughtlessly? wondered Ryan. He knew he was drinking plonk. By contrast, when they played poker in his flat they were invariably served a vintage burgundy, frequently domaine bottled. But then he seldom missed a chance to underline how well he was doing in the world.

.   .   .   .

Nina climbed into bed, but remained sitting up. 'Isn't it about time you started hearing from all the firms you've written to?' she asked.

Ryan untied his tie and hung it on the expanding wire rail on the inside of the wardrobe door. 'It's only a fortnight now, since I started applying for jobs.'

'But that's surely plenty of time for them to answer? What about that plastics firm in London who wanted a P.R.O.? The job was obviously made for you.'

'Maybe their typist is away with the 'flu,' he answered lightly. He took off his suit and hung it on a wooden hanger.

32

'I hope someone gets a move on. The money Llanarchs gave you won't last very long . . .' She spoke more softly. 'I'm sorry I keep worrying you, Hilary, but I just can't help it even though I know it's really being stupid.'

He smiled at her. 'Of course you're going to worry. But on Monday the postman will deliver so many letters offering jobs we'll have a hell of a job deciding which one to accept.'

'There was an article in the paper today.' She fidgeted with the edge of the sheet. 'It said the conditions of employment in this country are becoming more and more fluid and that inevitably there are going to be more redundancies and the older people will be lucky to get jobs of equal pay and opportunities.'

'Older people means men in their late fifties who aren't all that hot in their jobs anyway.' He finished undressing and put on his pyjamas.

'I can't help worrying,' she said, for the second time.

Neither could he.

5

It had been a cold and wet winter and although it was now the middle of March there was still no break in the dreary succession of grey rain-racked days and the strong east winds. In bad weather, Rushton became a dismal town.

Ryan walked past the large store which had once been noted for its quality, but which now offered only cheap furniture. As Rushton had grown in size and become more industrialised, so its standards had dropped. Not that he should any longer be bewailing that fact. The cheaper, the better. He shivered, despite the thick overcoat he was wearing, and stared across the road at the first-floor offices of the Middlemarch Employment Agency. He tried to tell himself that it was only by chance he'd come up Middlemarch Road, but knew this was a lie. Then he assured himself he wouldn't go into the agency today, but knew he would once he'd overcome his sense of shame and bitter embarrassment. Until then, he'd have a coffee at the café, where he'd spent so much time plucking up his courage like a schoolboy summoned to authority.

The waitress immediately recognised him and asked if he wanted the usual? She brought him a white coffee and the bill. As he stirred sugar into the coffee, he thought with something akin to pain that it was incredible he should now have to be concerned with the fact he'd spent another eight pence. Five months ago, he wouldn't have thought twice if he'd spent eight pounds.

He opened the *Daily Telegraph* at the jobs vacant advertisements and found two jobs to suit his qualifications. He'd write to the firms, of course, but he no longer really expected even to be called to an interview: it seemed the country must be full of redundant P.R.O.s in their middle forties.

He noticed and read an article addressed to redundant executives. It counselled them to patience because they must inevitably experience difficulties in gaining re-employment and suggested they should not be too dogmatic about requiring a salary equal to their last. The writer of the article wasn't a redundant executive, for sure, or he'd have concentrated on by far the most difficult problem—how to keep one's self-respect when unemployed.

How did one face one's wife when the bills kept arriving and there was no money to pay them and she was getting more and more frightened because there seemed to be no future? How did one live with one's bank manager who was sympathetic but could not allow the overdraft to climb and climb? How did one live with one's building society, who demanded repayments on the dot? How, as a failure, did one live with oneself?

It was astonishing to remember their early, easy, assured optimism once the initial shock had passed. Everything must soon be all right—as if they had a personal fairy who'd wave a magic wand. Other people might be in trouble over a long period, but they couldn't possibly be: even a television programme on the unemployed executive had not shocked them into reality. Only time and growing

35

fear, worry, and self-contempt, had done that.

The first time he'd drawn the dole he'd been so ashamed of being seen by someone he knew he'd have worn a disguise if he'd had one. When he'd spoken to the clerk, giving his professional details, he'd tried to make out it was all very temporary and he was only drawing the money because he'd paid for the stamps over the years . . . The clerk had looked at him with tired and knowing eyes.

He finished the coffee, paid at the counter with a ten-pence piece, took the change and hurriedly walked out past the bowl left for tips, and crossed the road to the employment agency. The flight of wooden steps had very well-worn treads. The blonde Mrs. Stevens was in her middle thirties. She wore a wedding ring, but never mentioned her family and always looked sad except when she actually smiled, and he was convinced she was either separated, divorced, or a widow. She'd always been very kind to him, showing a genuine sympathy. Even though she'd seen him every working day of the past week and had given the same answer each time, she now told him there were no jobs suitable for him in a manner that suggested she was quite confident the next time he came along she'd have good news.

.   .   .   .   .

Edward Anderson had a second-floor flat in a new block which had been built four years previously and stood in the centre of landscaped gardens. Each flat had two reserved spaces in the basement car park and a lockable bin in the wine cellars. At all times there was a uniformed porter on duty in the large and luxuriously appointed entrance foyer and each man was the very soul of discretion.

Ryan arrived at six-thirty in the evening and the porter recognised him and smiled a greeting. There was a lift waiting and this took him up to a small landing, off which were two flats. Ryan rang the bell of the right-hand flat and heard the chimes inside.

'Well, well, what an unexpected pleasure, old man! Come right in and name your poison. And where's my favourite brunette, the woman I'd have married if you hadn't got there first? . . . Tell you what, you can have a look at a little painting. A chap I know who's a crook has just conned me into buying it. Simply throwing money away, of course.'

Ryan looked at the painting and said all the right things, praising Anderson for his taste and managing not to choke on the words: he made a point of expressing the certainty that it must appreciate dramatically in value.

They went into the sitting-room, designed by a local interior decorator who believed in contrasting and even conflicting colours. The suite of furniture had cost seven hundred pounds: the carpet, the only truly attractive feature, had cost three hundred. Anderson settled back in the bright red armchair and raised his glass. 'Here's the skin off your nose.' Just for a moment there was a wary expression on his sallow face.

Ryan, who had endlessly rehearsed the words in his mind, suddenly found he couldn't speak them and instead said: 'We hadn't seen you for some time and were wondering how you are?'

'I'm fine. Bit too busy, of course—fertilising my ulcer and compounding my cholesterol with too much

37

eating, drinking, smoking, and what keeps us young.'
He winked, then spoke in vague terms about his latest
business deal, referring with impressive casualness
to hundreds of thousands of pounds.

This talk of money prompted Ryan finally to speak
about the reason for his visit. 'Ted . . . You know
you once said to come to you for advice at any time?'

'Sure, sure.' Anderson emptied his glass. He stood
up and refilled it, but did not bother to ask Ryan
if he would like another drink.

'I . . . I'd be very grateful for some help.'

'Nothing easier, old boy. Just tell me your problem
and I'll give you the solution, free, gratis, and for
nothing, tax deductible, and I can't do fairer than
that, can I?' He returned to his chair, sat down, and
lit a cigar.

In halting terms, Ryan said that finding another
job was proving far more difficult than he'd imagined
possible: it seemed a barrier came down as soon as
one was forty. Things, frankly, were getting a bit
tight. Was there someone amongst all Ted's very
wealthy and influential friends who might be able to
help and turn up a job—any sort of a job?

Anderson was very sympathetic. If only he could
have done, he'd have worked his knees to the bone
to help. But business was bloody tight. Everyone he
knew was in some sort of trouble. His own financial
problems were so acute that he didn't know whether
to go public, go bankrupt, or cut his throat with a
carving knife. But, naturally, if he ever heard of anything he'd pass on the news with the speed of light.

When Ryan left, Anderson was enjoying his
fourth very large whisky and his second cigar.

.   .   .   .   .

In their sitting-room, Nina stared at Ryan. 'But he said he'd help you any time, you'd only to ask.'

'I know,' he muttered.

'And he's a friend.'

She'd always had a naive belief in the essential goodness of other people, he thought, as he slumped back in the armchair.

'He surely could do at least something for you?'

'If he wanted to, yes.'

'Then what really happened?' Her voice quickened. 'Why didn't he want to? Were you rude to him, all sardonic as you can get, just because he's a bit vulgar?'

'He was simply being bloody-minded and you can't blame me for that. He was born like it.'

'I suppose you just couldn't hide your feelings. You had to show how superior you were.'

'I didn't get down on hands and knees and lick his boots, if that's what you really mean.'

Their pointless, angry rows, based on fear, were getting more and more frequent.

She blinked rapidly. 'But he said he'd help you.'

He suddenly needed a drink. He went across to the cocktail cabinet, but found there was nothing left other than three empty bottles and a tonic. He wondered if they'd any money in the house to go and buy a half-bottle of gin at the pub?

'If he ever came here and said he was in trouble, I'd do everything I could to help him,' she said.

'I know.' His voice was suddenly soft. That was the truth: she'd always help the lame, the blind, the needy. But it seemed to be a law of life that those who could help, wouldn't, and those who would, couldn't. He went over to the settee, sat down, and held her hand. The room was beginning to get uncomfortably cool because they were strictly rationing the coal they used.

The telephone rang. Reluctantly, he released her hand and stood up. When they couldn't pay the next quarter's bills, presumably the company would come and cut them off. The telephone was on a small triangular wooden shelf to the side of the stairs.

'Mr. Ryan? My name is Smith and I'm ringing on behalf of my firm, Pauls Carriers. I hope you don't mind me calling you at this time of night?'

'Of course not.' He tried to remember if the name should mean anything to him.

'I understand you've recently been made redundant after several years with Llanarch Motors?'

'Yes, that's right.' Hope suddenly began to thump in his chest.

'Would you tell me if you've yet found further employment?'

He automatically lied. 'I haven't found quite what I want, but I've a couple of interviews lined up.'

'Then at the moment you are free. Would you be interested in some well-paid part-time work?'

How to answer yes without showing too much eagerness? 'What kind of work would this be?'

'We're a firm who've specialised for many years in transporting small items which are too valuable to be moved by any of the ordinary means. By the very nature of this work, the people we employ must be completely honest, responsible, and possessed of considerable initiative—which is why we always employ executives such as yourself who are temporarily between regular jobs.'

'Where's your head office?'

'In central London, but in the normal course of events we don't have to bother you to come here. What happens is that you make contact with one of our staff at a pre-designated meeting place. We've found this is far the safest method of working and it offers a hundred per cent security. From your point of view, the advantage of this system is that you are paid when you hand over the item, or items, so there's no waiting for the money.' There was a quick chuckle. 'And as I said before, the fees we pay are very generous.'

'I see.' He didn't, but the words 'very generous' filled most of his mind.

'Then are you interested, Mr. Ryan?'

'Yes. Yes, I am.'

'Good. I'll contact you again as soon as we have a delivery to be made. Please remember, the one golden rule is that you tell no one what you're doing so that our security remains watertight.'

'But . . . but what about an interview?'

'Which will tell me no more than I already know from the fact you've been with so large a firm for so long. No, Mr. Ryan, you've no need to convince me that you're completely honest and trustworthy.' The connexion was cut.

Ryan slowly replaced the receiver. Some of the odder aspects of the conversation only now occurred to him, but he mentally shrugged them aside. He'd been offered a job that paid well. In his present desperate financial state, he'd have stood on his head and barked like a dog if that made money.

This must be the first break. His luck had changed.

6

Ryan crossed the main hall of Charing Cross station to the Smith news-stand in the centre and looked at the vast assortment of magazines that ranged in content from girls with visible charms to model railway building. Not for the first time, he wondered if the whole thing was a joke, played by one of his friends with a hitherto unsuspected cruel sense of humour. How could any firm employ him without personally interviewing him, more especially when his job apparently called for absolute integrity? And what about the directions for the meeting? Beneath the big clock with a rolled-up copy of *The Times* under his left arm and reply to the greeting by saying Pauls Carriers and Mr. Smith—shades of Soviet spy drops with the details of the latest atomic submarine. Joke or not, he'd had to come because of those words 'very well paid'.

He bought a copy of *The Times*, something he hadn't done in years. Headlines spoke of a strike in steelworks in the north in support of a hundred and twenty men declared redundant. His sympathy was now wholeheartedly with the strikers, not, as it would have been five months before, with the management.

He'd been directed to buy a ticket for Ashford, but hadn't, in case this was all a joke. He left the news-stand and crossed to the large clock, with its faces set at an angle, and stood under it, *The Times* beneath his left arm.

A woman walked towards him. She was dressed in a fashionably short skirt and wore very obvious make-up, so that she had a brassy look about her. Years ago, he would unhesitatingly have labelled her a tart and known he was right, but modern fashion made it impossible to be so certain. 'Mr. Ryan?' she asked.

'That's right, and you're from Pauls Carriers and Mr. Smith?'

She smiled. 'Here we are, then. One small package.' She handed him a brown paper package, sealed with Sellotape and string, six inches by three.

'When you arrive in Ashford, go to the public library and stand by the A fiction shelves. When someone asks you if you're Mr. Ryan, make the same answer as you did to me. Hand over this package. You'll be given your money there.'

'Look, what . . . ?'

'Goodbye, Mr. Ryan.' She turned and walked briskly away and soon was lost amongst a knot of passengers who were being ushered around by a flustered man with a mop of unruly white hair.

There was very little time in which to buy a ticket and catch the train. He ran into the booking hall, made icy through draft, and found a queue of several people at the only open second-class booking counter. He went to the first-class counter and found he hadn't enough money for a return so bought a single. He ran to platform number six and was waved through the barrier by the collector, who didn't bother to clip the ticket, as the whistle was blown. The train began to move as he scrambled into the last carriage. After stumbling over someone's feet, and apologising, he made his way along the

43

train to the first-class carriage. In the compartment in which he sat down there was only one other occupant, a very large woman, dressed in a tweedy suit that unsubtly emphasised her girth, wearing a great deal of jewellery, who continually fondled a Cavalier King Charles Spaniel with bulging eyes and matted coat.

He stared at the parcel and wondered just what in the hell was going on? Even if the handing of the parcel to him was best done in a public place, surely he could have expected to be ordered to deliver it to the client at the client's office and not to someone in a public library who had to be identified by passwords? He felt the package for weight and pressed the sides gently, examined all six sides, and learned nothing. He reached into his coat pocket for a pack of cigarettes.

'This is a no-smoking compartment,' said the woman.

Silently swearing, he replaced the pack.

'It's not that I mind,' she continued, pronouncing it maynd, 'it's just that this is a no-smoking compartment. And as I always say, the world goes round more smoothly when we all do as we're told. Don't you agree?'

He agreed. Dismally, he guessed she was going to go on and on talking and he was right. The words gushed out in an endless stream for the whole hour the journey took: from time to time, even the panting dog was called upon to pass comment.

They drew into Ashford. Doors clattered open and muffled announcements over the P.A. system explained which platforms passengers should go to for connecting trains on branch lines.

44

The stream of disembarked passengers went up stairs and past the ticket collector. Ryan found himself in an enclosed area which housed booking counters, newsagent, telephones, and offices, and had an exit at either end. He left by the right-hand one and descended stairs to the outside and a car park. There was a light drizzle coming down from the leaden sky and everything was dirtily wet.

Three taxis were drawn up at the rank and he went across to the first. 'Can you tell me, please, where the public library is?'

'Up the road and through the park,' replied the moon-faced man, ill-tempered at not getting a fare.

Ryan began to walk. There was a pub and then a garage with a multi-storey building and showroom filled with glossy new cars. In front ot the showroom were a few second-hand cars for sale, including a Llanarch Dubhe—notorious for providing more warranty work than any other car on the market. He stared at it, not really seeing it but remembering that he'd had to sell his Llanarch three weeks ago at a knock-down price in order to pay off some of the more pressing debts. That had been their last asset of value except for the house, and much of that belonged to the mortgage company. He walked on, frightened because the sight of the car had reminded him of something—he and Nina could get no closer to financial disaster without tumbling right into it.

The park looked neat but forlorn in the grey drizzle, the kind of place used but seldom enjoyed. As he left it, he saw on the far side of the road a new building which he correctly identified as the public library.

Inside was warmth and typical low-key hum of sound, murmured conversations, shuffling feet, the snapping of books.

He located the A fiction shelves, against the wall and to the left and below short stories—listed as Anthologies, perhaps?—and looked at the books. Acton, Amis, Alding, Armstrongs of many initials: some authors he'd read and liked or disliked, some he'd never heard of.

'Mr. Ryan?'

She was about the same age as the woman at Charing Cross and dressed in the same tarty fashion, yet her smile was warm and pleasant and suggested a softer character. 'Yes. And you're from Pauls Carriers and Mr. Smith?'

'That's it. Did everything go O.K.?'

'Yes, thanks.'

'Fine. Then let me have the package, will you?'

He gave her the package.

'This is yours, Mr. Ryan, and Mr. Smith said to tell you that there'll probably be another job in three days' time if you want it.' She handed him a sealed brown envelope. 'Goodbye.'

He watched her. She walked past the checking-out counter, through the doors into the lobby, and out on to the street and didn't look back.

For some reason he deliberately did not try to analyse, he didn't immediately open the envelope to see how much they'd paid him, but instead went into the reference room and sat down at one of the tables, next to two schoolgirls who were giggling over a book.

He made certain no one was watching through the glass windows of the main library, then slit the envelope with his thumb. Inside were five five-pound notes.

Twenty-five pounds was a hell of a lot for what he'd done, even if the firm did need men of unimpeachable integrity. But, he tried to assure himself, integrity always cost. Why didn't they use registered post, which would have been so very much cheaper? But regularly there were thefts of mail. Why had his contacts been in public places and not in offices? But obviously the chances of anyone's following through the consignment became virtually nil. What could the package have contained to be worth so high a transportation fee? Jewellery collected from a bank, industrial papers worth a fortune to any competitor ...

Twenty-five pounds was a considerable sum to anyone who was having trouble collecting together twenty-five pence. He slowly put the envelope into his breast pocket and stood up. One of the schoolgirls looked at him and then giggled more than ever as her companion whispered something.

He left the library and, after directions from an elderly woman, walked past the church to the main street which showed very obvious signs of the modernisation which had robbed it of any character: just like Rushton, he thought, ever-booming quantity, ever-disappearing quality. He searched for and eventually found an old-style family grocer and bought a pot of Danish 'caviar' which Nina liked so much, but which they had not been able to afford for months.

7

Nina put two pieces of bread in the pop-up toaster and pressed down the central stud and the elements crackled as they heated up. She picked up the lemon from beside the jar of caviar and fiddled with it as she stared at him.

'Twenty-five pounds for taking a parcel from Charing Cross to Ashford just seems too much,' he said, his voice filled with uncertainty.

'But you knew from the beginning the job was well paid.'

He took a pack of cigarettes from his pocket and she sat down at the table and they smoked.

'Hilary, you've just told me how easily everything can be explained—their not wanting to use the post, the amount, the slightly odd way you met the people.'

'I know, but . . .' But how far did he believe his own explanations?

'Wouldn't they have given you much more than twenty-five pounds if there were anything really wrong? I mean, no one would do anything illegal for just that much.'

'I've thought of that,' he answered.

'But you don't agree?'

He stared at her desperately worried face. Twenty-five pounds meant she could pay some of the house-keeping bills: the chance of another job in three days' time meant that then more of them could be paid. How justified was he in continuing to query the way things had gone? Hadn't he found perfectly logical explanations for everything? Wasn't it just being perverse to worry, when there was no other job open to him? It was Pauls Carriers or nothing. And nothing meant no more money and Nina would continue to be tortured by worry and then he'd be mentally crucified because he couldn't stand seeing her so distressed. 'You're dead right, darling.'

The toaster popped up, startling them both. She picked out the toast and began to butter it. 'You really do think it's all all right? That if there were anything wrong, they'd obviously pay a lot more?'

'Yes.' And now he did.

.   .   .   .   .

The blonde Mrs. Stevens at the Middlemarch Employment Agency stopped work and smiled at him. 'Hullo, Mr. Ryan. It's a bit of a better day, isn't it?'

'It certainly is. If the weatherman's not careful, we'll wake up one morning and find it's actually spring. What kind of a trip did you have to Oxford?'

'Not too bad except the train was late arriving, which upset things a bit. Still, it was nice once we arrived. So wonderful to see all the old colleges— like meeting history face-to-face, I always say.'

'I'm so glad you had a good time in the end.' From the start, he'd chatted her up because a carefully developed contact might just pay dividends: there could be a job going and she would immediately think of him first. A man learned a basic cunning and shed most of his self-respect when he was desperate. 'I just dropped in, Mrs. Stevens, to see if anything's stirring?'

She shook her head and looked vaguely apologetic. 'I'm sorry, Mr. Ryan, but there just doesn't seem to be anything that would suit you at the moment. But I'm sure there will be soon even if things are so difficult at the moment.'

Her expressed optimism would have sounded better without that final qualification, he thought. Suppose she told him the plain, unvarnished truth, would it be that he hadn't a snowball's chance in hell?

He spoke about general topics for a while, then said goodbye and left, going down the well-worn stairs to the road and the sunshine which brought a sense of cheer, if no warmth. He walked along the pavement. Smith of Pauls Carriers had said there'd probably be another job in three days' time, but that was now a week ago. Had it all fallen through? Was that second twenty-five pounds now only a mirage? He drew level with the men's outfitters where he'd sometimes bought suits. One of the two brothers who owned it was in the doorway and he smiled and wished Ryan a deferential good afternoon. The ironic similarity of the tailor's attitude towards him and his attitude towards Miss Stevens was not easily missed: was his assumed politeness as doomed to unproductiveness as was the tailor's?

He turned left at the traffic lights and went down Prestland Road in which were many old and mellow buildings, housing shops and offices that were scheduled for demolition because the area was to be redeveloped. At the bottom of the slight hill was a new complex of shops and offices that marked the site of the old market. He remembered the turmoil of market day, the snarled-up traffic, the stalls of cheap-jack goods, the bellowing of cattle, the bleating of sheep, the smell of dung, the farmers all looking slightly stiff and ill-at-ease in their best clothes: the memory was a nostalgic one because when the market had existed there he had been P.R.O. at Llanarch Motors and when he was short of money he merely twisted the bank manager's arm to jack up the overdraft.

The road turned left and here were large Victorian houses that were now doctors' and dentists' surgeries, commercial and council offices, and a betting shop. The employment exchange was in the last house. Even with a considerble stretch of the imagination there was no job for which he was suited.

Back in the High Street, he was about to go into a café for another cup of coffee when he stopped to check what he had on him. He could not find enough. The humiliation of his situation, even though known only to himself, filled him with a wild rage and despair in which he promised himself action he knew he'd never take. He walked on, very quickly, as if physical effort might help, round the square where a bronze Queen Victoria was not amused to be overlooking public lavatories and along the two miles to Thorndale House.

He opened the front gate, still squealing because he'd never got round to oiling it, and then stopped on the flagstone path. It was not a very exciting house from an architectural point of view, but it did look comfortable, the kind of place in which would live a happy family who enjoyed life. To be forced to move would be too painful for contemplation. Except it had to be contemplated.

Nina, knitting in right hand, met him in the hall. She was trying to make some money knitting for a

51

shop in Rushton, but had very soon discovered how ill-paid the work was.

He was the first to speak. 'Has anyone phoned?'

She shook her head. 'No. They've been no messages of any sort.'

He removed his overcoat and hung it on the old mahogany stand and immediately became aware of the chill in the hall because the radiator was not on. He'd intended to say nothing more, determined to give no hint of how worried he was, but the words seemed to speak themselves. 'The last thing the woman said was there'd be another job in three days' time. It's a week since then.'

'Maybe . . .' She passed the knitting over to her left hand in a purely nervous gesture.

'I did exactly as they told me to, so why haven't they been on to me? We've got to have more money.'

She seemed to shiver. 'Come on, let's go into the sitting-room where there's a fire and I'll make you some coffee.'

The telephone rang an hour later, when he was looking through the jobs vacant advertisements for the third time, kidding himself he might have missed one that was relevant. He dropped the paper on to the floor and hurried out into the hall.

The caller was Smith. 'Mr. Ryan, are you free and willing to do another small job for us?'

'I think I will be, yes, but when exactly?' Automatically, he still spoke as if it were a strong possibility that a whole host of would-be employers were likely to descend on him.

'This coming Thursday.'

'Yes, I am free that day.'

'That's good. Now we want you to go to Paris this time—I suppose you've a valid passport?'

'Yes, I have.' Ryan saw Nina step into the hall. She watched him, hopeful yet frightened things could still go wrong.

'You're to collect a package in Paris and bring it back. We'll send you the tickets by post for travelling by Skyways, spending one night at the Hotel Croisette in Rue Carnot. At eleven o'clock Friday morning go to the Café Le Béarne which is nearby in the Place Guy Coquille. Have you got that?'

'Give me the last two names again, will you?' he asked, as he wrote rapidly on the telephone pad.

Smith repeated the names. 'Have a pleasant trip, Mr. Ryan. I'm sure we'll be able to work together a lot, most profitably for both of us. Goodbye.'

Nina spoke as Ryan replaced the receiver. 'Well?'

'I'm off to Paris on Thursday and it sounds like plenty of work after that.'

'And did they say if they'd pay the same each time?'

He shook his. 'He didn't mention payment. But it can't be any less, can it?'

'I shouldn't think so.' She came and touched him with her left hand and kissed him on the cheek. 'I know it may not be the kind of work you like doing, darling, but it is earning some money.'

He nodded. Money was the only important thing now because if ever he were unable to keep the house going he'd cease to feel he was a husband or even a man.

8

For Ryan, Paris was always the siren, beckoning and then disappointing. In the past, he wondered why and had sardonically come to the conclusion that in his heart he naively expected the city to be as reputation would have it, full of adventure and romantic affairs for every man with red blood in his veins. Even experience didn't seem to dim this expectation, freshly nurtured for every visit. Not, ironically, that he'd ever have taken advantage of a languorous, lascivious blonde: from the day he'd married Nina he'd never slept with another woman, although on two well-remembered occasions he'd undeniably been offered the opportunity.

Friday morning was clear of cloud and the sun shone, though with little warmth to combat the continuing north-east wind. Ryan left the Hotel Croisette, a small family hotel which was fresh and clean but without any touch of luxury, and walked up to the cross-roads where the lights were against his crossing. He waited as the traffic roared past, every motorist engaged in battle. What would this job be worth? Perhaps more than the last, as it was a longer one? Fifty pounds would make a hell of a difference back home.

The lights changed and the last motorist rushed wildly past. Ryan crossed between the studs, remembering his mother's advice always to do so, because although the Parisian motorist was still very likely to knock one down, there would be some compensation for one's heir's. His mother had frequently known what it was like to be really hard up, yet he could never remember this having visibly affected her. Her philosophy had been simple. If the milkman couldn't be paid today, he might be able to be paid tomorrow: the more you owed a tradesman, the more eager he was to continue serving you in order—hopefully—eventually to be paid all his debts.

The Café Le Béarne was on the south side of the Place Guy Coquille, close to the Boulevard Malesherbes. It was small, unpretentious, and for Parisians not tourists: behind the rough counter was a vast array of bottles and a proprietor who looked as if he sampled most of them, in front were four bare-topped tables each with a couple of chairs. On the walls were fly-blown mirrors, official notices against drunkenness, and a number of out-of-date posters advertising catch.

Two men at the counter were playing with dice, loudly exclaiming over each throw. When Ryan entered they momentarily looked up, expressions surly, then they resumed playing and speaking so rapidly that Ryan, who knew a little French, failed to understand one word in six. Typically, the proprietor showed his sturdy independence by ignoring Ryan for a while, then moved down quickly to serve him in case his independence should result in a lost customer. Ryan ordered Cinzano. He had to repeat the order twice, varying the pronounciation, before the proprietor was prepared to understand him. A Parisian peasant, his mother had always said with rare malice and recognising the contradiction in terms, was one of the rudest persons on earth.

Ryan carried the well-filled glass over to the table

nearest the large window and sat down. To pass the time, he watched the traffic and after a few minutes saw a Riga pass, looking extraordinarily tatty even by Llanarch standards.

A man came into the bar, looked briefly at Ryan and said good morning in English, crossed to the bar and ordered a whisky in a French so fluent that the proprietor had no chance to pretend he couldn't understand. He came and sat down opposite Ryan. 'Here's health,' he said, as he raised his glass before drinking.

Ryan studied him. At first he appeared an ordinary man in his late twenties or early thirties, handsome in a rugged manner, lips too full, neatly dressed in a suit and short overcoat, but then Ryan noticed the flatness of his gaze and he suddenly became convinced the man was quite vicious in character.

'Was everything at the hotel all right?' The man spoke with a nasal twang.

'Yes, thanks. The place is comfortable and the road's not too busy at night.' Ryan lit a cigarette. It seemed to him he was being summed-up, as if some final decision were being taken.

The man produced a small package, wrapped in brown paper, and placed it on the table between them. 'This is to go to London on the afternoon flight.'

There was clearly something more to be said and Ryan waited.

'It's a diamond ring. We'd rather it wasn't declared when you go into England.'

'You . . . you mean, you want it sumuggled in?'

The man smiled, showing even white teeth.

'But . . .' Ryan cut short the words. To claim he'd

56

no idea he was going to be asked to do something even vaguely illegal was rather ridiculous: from the first contact with Mr. Smith of Pauls Carriers he had basically suspected illegality of some sort, no matter how hard he'd tried to deny this to himself. But now that it was out in the open . . .

'I'll tell you a bit about the history,' said the man, in a confidential tone of voice. 'It's been left to Mr. Smith's daugher by a French relative. It's quite valuable and the duty would be more'n Mr. Smith could pay if it's properly declared. Duty like this is a bleeding imposition, so he's naturally doing what he can to avoid it.'

'But I'm pretty sure that when someone's left something in a will he'll probably be allowed to take it into England without paying duty if he proves what's happened—you know, show the will.'

The man studied Ryan, scooped the small parcel across the table and pocketed it. 'You're for forgetting the job? O.K. That's all right by me.'

Ryan drew on the cigarette.

The man finished his drink with a quick swallow, asked Ryan what his was, and went over to the bar. When he returned and passed the refilled glass over, he said: 'There's no call to look so glum, we're not ones to take offence if you reckon on out. You settle for your night in Paris which hasn't cost you a franc and leave us to worry about finding someone to do the job.'

Ryan cleared his throat. 'This ring . . .' He stopped.

The man leaned back in his chair and drank.

Ryan spoke hurriedly. 'It's not stolen, or anything like that?'

The man grinned widely. 'Jesus! D'you reckon me on being a villain? A half-chiv in each hand and a shooter in the pocket?'

Ryan stubbed out one cigarette and immediately lit another. He remembered how desperately Nina—and, for that matter, he—was relying on the money.

The man finished his whisky with a quick tilt of the glass, which he put down with a slight thump on the Ricard mat. 'There's nothing stopping you staying a while—the air firm'll change your ticket. If you go for stripping, try the new place in Pigalle called the Petite Poulette—they reckon it gives even Soho a run for its money.'

Ryan cleared his throat. 'I'll take it,' he said, his voice hoarse.

'You'll what?'

'I'll deliver the package to London.'

'Yeah? Well, I ain't so certain on that.'

'But you said that's what you wanted.'

'Sure. And you said no. When a guy backs out, that's the time to call a halt. You don't want to do a quick bit of smuggling for the director's daughter—that'll all right by everyone. If a man wants to stay all legal and give up a century in cash, that's his decision. But when it comes to changing the mind . . .' He took a pack of Gitanes from his pocket and lit one.

'How much did you say?' demanded Ryan.

'A century, a hundred, seein' the job's out of the usual line of things.'

Ryan spoke urgently. 'I only said no because it was an automatic reaction.'

'Because you ain't ever before smuggled anything but a packet of fags?'

Ryan nodded. 'But then it's not as if this is anything . . . well . . .'

'Big time? No, it's not that.' The man flashed his grin again.

'Is it all right, then, if I carry on and take the ring through to London?'

The man hesitated.

'I . . . I really could do with the money.'

He brought the envelope back out of his pocket. 'O.K., you've sold me—so remember, no sweating as you pass through Customs! When you arrive, go to Piccadilly underground at seven and wait by that map of the world which shows the times in each country.' He drained his glass and stood up, moving with the litheness of trained muscles, said goodbye, and left.

Ryan dropped the ring into his pocket. Smuggling was officially a criminal activity, but most travellers had at some time indulged in it and never thought of it as any sort of a crime—and what could be less harmful than to take to a man's daughter the ring she had been left in a will?

.   .   .   .   .

The aeroplane touched down at Lympne airport, taxied along to the disembarking area in front of a low huddle of buildings. The whine of the turbo-prop motors died away. Steps were wheeled up, the door opened, and the hostess, a blonde with turned-up nose and eyes which said she was always on the look-out, smilingly said goodbye to each passenger.

In the Customs shed, with no special pass out point for those with nothing to declare, Ryan put his suit-

59

case on the low search bench and tried to think of anything but sweating. He thought he felt sweat prickle his face. The ring, now in the breast pocket of his coat, seemed to bulge unmistakably.

Standing next in line was an elderly clergyman, white-haired and very venerable-looking, all toothy smiles and polite denials when asked if he'd anything to declare. He was told to open his brief-case and two suitcases and all were thoroughly searched. The Customs officer looked faintly surprised when he found nothing, then moved down to stand opposite Ryan. He asked if the suitcase was all the luggage, jerked his head towards the exit, and it was several seconds before Ryan realised he was free to carry on.

The coach journey from Lympne to the terminal in Elizabeth Street, by Victoria coach station, was fairly quick, with traffic light until actually in London. Rain started when they reached Eltham and by the time they disembarked it was drizzling with dismal monotony.

After passing the intervening time in a café where he ate a stale pastry and half drank a cup of very peculiar-tasting coffee, Ryan went down into Picadilly underground station and round to the time map of the world. He stared at the passing people, sometimes trying to fit character to faces, often depressed by the large number whose expressions spoke overwhelmingly of discontent.

A woman came directly towards him and he immediately recognised her from their previous meeting at Charing Cross station. She smiled, but without warmth, and spoke no more than a dozen words as he gave her the package and in return she handed him an envelope with a hundred pounds in it.

.   .   .   .   .

Nina was in an ambivalent state of mind, delighted he should have been paid as much as a hundred pounds, troubled by what he'd done because she loved him too sincerely to view with equanimity the slightest danger to him. 'I . . . I rather wish you'd refused to bring the ring over,' she said.

He looked across the dining-room table as he ate the late supper she had prepared for him. 'I know what you mean, but it was only handling a ring which was the girl's anyway: that's not really smuggling at all.'

'But it was, wasn't it?'

He shook his head and smiled. 'Five per cent smuggling, maybe, and that's being generous.' He suddenly remembered how her mother had once told him that Nina could never do anything she knew for certain to be wrong because of her over-active conscience.

She gestured vainly with her hands.

'We've got to be strictly practical,' he said bluffly.

She couldn't stop arguing around her own fears. 'Six months ago you wouldn't have done it.'

'Six months ago I had a job,' he replied with sudden bitterness, 'and I was of some use.'

'Don't talk like that. Whatever happens, you mean everything to me.'

It was ironic that in smuggling the ring in order to ease her fears, he'd raised fresh fears—yet he had no compunctions or regrets about what he'd done.

As he'd said, the smuggling had been a virtually harmless act and the hundred pounds meant so much to them.

.   .   .   .   .

Anderson leaned back in his chair in the sitting-room of Thorndale House. 'You know something—it's great to be back for our game of poker. Say, what happened to your collection of decanter labels that used to be in the cupboard over there?'

'We sold them.' Ryan, refilling all their glasses, wondered how any man could be so insensitively gauche? Had he completely forgotten Ryan's visit to ask for help?

Polly Comyns, indignant at Anderson, rushing to overcome the effects of his words, said: 'I'm so glad things are more cheerful for both of you now. I really was terribly concerned.' She was a woman who genuinely did worry about other people. Starvation in Pakistan, floods in India, suffering in Jordan, a neighbour falling ill, distressed her to an unusual degree.

Comyns picked up the cards and with economical movements shuffled them into order.

Ryan returned to the table with his own glass and sat down. 'Cheers to all of us and may the devil never get a look in.'

Comyns dealt the cards.

'What is it you're doing now, Hilary?' asked Anderson. 'Are you a director of I.C.I.?' He laughed.

'I've found a part-time job as a messenger.' Ryan picked up his cards and found he hadn't even a pair.

They bought cards: Anderson two, Ryan five, Polly one, Nina three, and Comyns three.

Polly didn't wait for the bidding, but threw her cards in, Nina did the same. Ryan passed, even though he had three threes. Anderson bet a blue chip. Comyns threw in. Ryan raised it a white chip.

'Look out, folks, we've got Rothschild playing against us,' said Anderson, with mock concern. He fanned out his cards. 'Now can I beat four kings? Tell you what—raise you.' He added two green chips, making it the maximum raise of forty pence.

Looking at Anderson, Ryan knew a sudden hatred for the other who throughout the evening had shown a complete lack of tact—at the beginning, he'd noisily turned down Polly's delicately made suggestion they lower the stakes—and now, typically, was raising forty pence because he reckoned that would frighten Ryan off unless he had a thumping good hand.

Ryan looked again at his three threes. He threw in.

'Well, well! It's a good job no one was willing to have a look at what I'd got,' said Anderson, with a deep satisfaction he did not try to hide.

.   .   .   .   .

Ryan and Nina went up to bed just after midnight. When she came into bed, he embraced her and soon was caressing her, but she said she was sorry she was really tired and had a bit of a head. He moved away.

He was sorry she no longer enjoyed sex as she had in the early days of their marriage, but recently he'd become less resentful of the fact. Perhaps his resigned acceptance was the first sign of real middle age.

The telephone rang.

She dropped the book she'd been reading. 'Who on earth can that be?'

Because of the unusually late hour of the call, he knew she immediately and instinctively sensed disaster: in the flick of an eyelid, she had thought up some of the worst things which could happen to them.

The caller was Smith. 'Sorry to bother you, it being so late, but we've a rush job. Would you be all right for New York on Tuesday?'

'I suppose so,' he answered, momentarily uncertain simply because it had not occurred to him he would ever be asked to go so far.

'Don't forget a visa. Be in the departure lounge of the T.W.A. building at ten o'clock.'

Nina called out, her voice high with fear. 'Who is it? Is anything wrong?'

9

Passengers in the T.W.A. lounge wandered about restlessly, as people about to go on long journeys so often did, and watches were continuously being consulted: there was a regular traffic downstairs to the cloakrooms, especially by parents with small children. At the reception counter, uniformed staff somehow remained good-humoured as they answered the same questions over and over again.

Ryan looked at his watch. Half an hour to departure time of the coach and still no one had made contact with him. He smoked another cigarette, although his mouth was already beginning to taste like yesterday's washing-up water. This flight to New York disturbed him, for a reason he couldn't pinpoint. . . .

He saw the woman he'd met in Ashford public library come through the outside doors into the lounge. He failed to notice that she did not have to look round for where he was, but came straight over. She was wearing a well-made leather coat over a smart, short dress and knee-length leather boots of beautiful quality and her make-up was more subtle than before so that she could easily have passed as fashionable: when she smiled and said hullo, how was he?, she appeared innocently young. She sat down on the other side of the small round table.

Ryan looked up at the wall clock and spoke nervously: 'Have you got the tickets? I haven't checked in yet.'

She took an envelope and a small package from her very large black leather handbag. 'Here are the tickets with a hundred dollars for expenses.' She handed him the envelope. 'And this is what you're to deliver.' She put the package, neatly wrapped in plain brown paper, two inches square by four inches, in the middle of the table. 'By the way . . .' She winked. 'I'm to tell you to slip it through as neatly as you did the ring. O.K.?'

'Yes,' he said, wishing he had the strength of character to refuse.

'You're lucky, going to New York. I've always wanted to go there. Apart from anything else, we get paid on a time-away basis. That's why I keep putting in for Japan—but I never get further than Manchester. Unfair to women's lib, I say.'

He forgot his doubts and began to speculate on how much this trip would be worth? If they'd paid a hundred pounds for the time away on the Paris trip . . .

'You're booked in at the Mount Royal Hotel in East Twenty-second Street. At five this afternoon, go along to the first bookshop in West Forty-seventh Street, which runs between Broadway and Eighth Avenue north of Times Square, and wait by the end slot machine. Have you got all that?'

'I'll just write it down . . .'

'Don't write anything down, remember it. Mount Royal Hotel. West Forty-seventh Street. Five o'clock.' She stood up.

He watched her leave, hips swinging sufficiently to make them interesting. Then he carried his suitcase across to the nearest checking-in point where it was weighed and ticketed and he was allocated his plane seat. 'Thank you, Mr. Ryan. The bus will be leaving in ten minutes. We'll be calling you when it's ready.'

He returned to his seat and lit yet another cigarette. He felt the packet in the pocket of his mackintosh. Since he was being asked to smuggle again there could be no doubting the essential dishonesty of the firm, but he comforted himself with the thought that there was little harm done. Then his mind returned to the question of how much he might reasonably expect for this trip.

·   ·   ·   ·   ·

The American Customs were hardly interested in him. He had to open his suitcase, but was told to shut it almost immediately, and his mackintosh, carried over his arm, was ignored.

He took a cab from the airport. The driver was untraditionally morose and said little on the journey, made long by the press of traffic which increased heavily as soon as they crossed East River. The hotel staff were efficient, checking him in within thirty seconds, but not troubling to welcome him, and the Puerto Rican bellhop appeared to be satisfied with the dollar tip. The room was reasonably sized and overlooked a very small paved courtyard ten storeys below, the television didn't work, a notice on the wall offered room service at near astronomical prices when translated into pounds, and the bathroom had some cracked tiles on the floor and a cold tap to the bath which dripped no matter how tightly it was shut. It was a hotel for non-executives and English visitors.

He sat on one of the twin beds and checked on the time, regretfully decided it was too early to have a drink. Then he thought how absurd it was that he should have smuggled in a parcel and so broken the law, yet would not now allow himself a drink which was perfectly legal simply because he still partially lived by the precepts his parents had taught him, one of which was that no gentleman ever drank in the middle of the afternoon because that was the first step towards drunkenness. A conscience could clearly be at one and the same time very elastic and quite unyielding.

He left the hotel and walked up Madison Avenue to 44th Street and then along to Times Square. New York was a city that both intrigued and baffled him. He was excited by the soaring skyscrapers, yet was depressed by them because they were so strictly functional and without any romance of restful age: the rush of life charged him with a sense of constructive urgency, yet everywhere there were obvious examples of the utter indifference to the drop-out and it was impossible to imagine there could be room here for the pleasant, amusing, but ineffectual intellectual who was part of the London scene.

Times Square had changed little since he had last seen it, on a trip to introduce to the States the Llanarch 1500 c.c. Hamal: Americans had shown their inate common sense by ignoring the car. Only the stores and cinemas dealing in pornography seemed to have increased. And it was a pornographic bookshop in West Forty-seventh Street to which he had been sent.

Pornography always amused and only occasionally excited him and in a patronisingly superior manner he'd always presumed that that was because a happy marriage insulated him from it. Nevertheless, some of the glossy colour magazines on display did make him wonder if perhaps he hadn't wasted much of his youth in true innocence.

The slot machines were in a darkened section at the back of the shop. Built like large juke-boxes, they offered a variety of films at a quarter a showing. He inserted a quarter in the end machine and punched at random one of the buttons. The small screen lit up and a very worn film began. The two ladies were evidently very great friends indeed.

'You like it?' asked a voice.

He turned. The speaker was a coloured man in his middle thirties. He wore a black leather coat, decorated with brass punch-buttons, and jeans. He had a small beard, bloodshot eyes, and a flattened nose.

'You'd be Mr. Ryan—right?' He spoke in a softly pitched voice that somewhere deep within it held a note of viciousness.

'Yes, that's right.' Ryan suddenly felt absurd, watching a poor, shoddy pornographic film.

'So where do you live?'

'In England.'

'Man, you surprise me!'

Ryan flushed. 'What I mean is . . .'

'What's the name of your house, Mr. Ryan?'

'Thorndale House. But what does that matter?'

'And the street and town?'

'Gerard Street, in Rushton. But surely . . . ?'

'Just checking. Have you brought over anything from London?'

'I've a small parcel for you.'

'Then give, man.'

He became more nervous and when he tried to get the package out of his mackintosh pocket his hand clumsily caught in the lining so that there was a short struggle before he pulled it out. He passed it over.

'So now, Mr. Ryan, you'd like what's yours?' He handed Ryan a large envelope. 'Enjoy your films, man. They say they're great.' He turned and left, walking with lithe grace.

Ryan shoved the envelope into his breast pocket, still angry that he should have appeared to be a dirty middle-aged man after a cheap thrill. He left the shop, passing all the men with rapt, sometimes strained, expressions who browsed through magazines and books and went out into the street where the keen wind seemed even keener after the stuffy warmth he had just left.

Back in Times Square and next to one of the few cinemas showing ordinary commercial films, he went into a café where he ordered a whisky and griddle cake with syrup. The whisky came first and restored much of his composure. Just what the hell did it matter if he had been watching one of the porn (or should it be corn?) films and the coloured man had shown amused contempt?

The waiter was clearing a nearby table and Ryan called for a second whisky. While he waited, he took the envelope from his coat pocket and slit open the flap. There were a number of notes inside and because he wasn't used to American currency it took him a little time to realise they added up to two thousand five hundred dollars.

Quite suddenly, he was terrified. No one paid just over a thousand pounds for petty smuggling. He'd been caught up in something really vicious.

10

Nina greeted him in the hall and kissed him hullo, then led him into the sitting-room. 'You look so tired, darling. Sit down and I'll get you a long, strong drink. You must be absolutely worn out.'

As she finished speaking, the old grandfather clock in the hall, one of the few things to come from his parents home, struck midnight.

He sat down in his armchair and stared at the fire, now almost burnt out. Waves of tiredness and frightened depression swept through his mind.

'There we are.' She handed him a glass of whisky that was at full strength. 'By the time you've finished that, I expect you'll be singing Rule Britannia!' She sat on the arm of his chair, leaned against him, and put her hand on his neck. 'Guess what?' Her voice was excited.

He belatedly realised that she was unusually cheerful and obviously had something to impart. 'You tell me.'

'There was a telephone call yesterday.'

For once, her playful way of drawing out the news irritated him. With a perversity that was rooted in his own troubles, he refused to ask her about the call.

'Aren't you the least bit interested?' she teased. 'But of course, you're so tired—I forgot. Darling, it was Mrs. Stevens.'

'Who?' He was still only half concentrating on what she was saying.

'Mrs. Stevens, from the Middlemarch Employment place. She was so disappointed when she heard you were away—I didn't say you were in New York or it might have sounded as if you weren't really hard up and in need of a job, mightn't it? She says there's a job all lined up for you as P.R.O. with a small firm who specialise in G.T. cars and who have started racing. Their name's Drew—does that mean anything to you? I thought I recognised the name.'

'Yes, it means a lot.' His voice quickened. 'How definite is the job?'

'As near as it can be before you go for an interview. Mrs. Stevens says she's been specially looking out for you because you're so charming—do I have a rival? For heaven's sake, darling, remember to go and thank her with flowers or an enormous box of chocolates. The moment she saw the vacancy for an experienced P.R.O., she thought of you. The salary's almost a thousand less than you were getting at Llanarch, but we can economise.'

'My God, we can!' he muttered.

'Isn't it thrilling?'

'Coming out of the blue like this, it's a genuine miracle.'

'So now there's no need to look like you did when you stepped into the house just now—as if someone had just told you your funeral was tomorrow.'

'We'd better not raise the flag too soon. I've still got to survive the interview. Don't forget, they may want a younger man, like so many firms do.'

When she really wanted something to happen, she became wildly and blindly optimistic. 'Mrs. Stevens says you age is O.K.—the firm are looking for a mature man. So you're in. You are mature, aren't

72

you?' She laughed. 'Heavens! I've been burbling on and I never asked how your trip went?'

'All right.'

'Did they pay as much as you hoped?'

'Three hundred dollars,' he lied, determined to hide the truth.

'How much is that in pounds?'

'Just over a hundred and twenty.'

'Then it wasn't quite as much as you thought it might be—but what the hell!' She suddenly became serious. 'It wasn't smuggling again, was it?'

'I . . . I shouldn't think so, no.'

'Thank God for that! I hated your doing that sort of thing. Let's forget it all now—it's the past. Just think, Hilary, you'll be back at work and all the awful times will only be a memory. Shall I tell you something? I've made a special pact with myself. I'm not going to spend another penny on luxuries. . . . At least, not until we're absolutely straight again.'

He emptied his glass and stood up. 'All this calls for another drink for both of us.'

'It's a bit late.'

'It's never too late.'

'As the bishop said to the actress on his ninety-first birthday.' She giggled. 'I learnt that at school when I didn't understand what it really meant.'

He poured out the drinks and returned to his seat. He felt light-headed. After months of misery and mental anguish, during which he'd continually made excuses for his own actions in order to hide the truth, he'd reached the end of the road and his troubles were all but over.

.   .   .   .   .

By international standards, the Drew Motoring Company was virtually insignficant, but to all car enthusiasts it was very well known. Stanley Drew had taken his degree at Imperial College, London, and then worked for one of the major motor manufacturers. He was in many ways a genius, intolerant of compromise. His work was original and creative and this, together with his inability to settle for second best, ensured he was sacked after eighteen stormy months.

Most men of twenty-six, sacked from their first job, would have tried to rebuild their self-respect, learn from experience, and find another job where they could better fit in with the organisation. Drew, with a kind of magnificent contempt for possibilities, said he'd start his own firm, making a car of honest quality and design. People laughed at him: as soon start digging for diamonds in Regent Street. Within one year his prototype 1500 c.c. fibreglass-bodied car with suspension partially based on current Formula One racing practice and partially on new ideas of his own was winning saloon car races against Lotus, Fords, and even transcontinental V8s, after two hears he had built a dozen more cars for drivers who went out and won races, after five years he owned a factory that was annually producing just under a thousand of the most desirable small G.T. cars in the world and for which there were impatient customers, and after six years he designed a Formula One car with bathtub monocoque chassis and his own suspension, used a Cosworth DFV engine and Hewland gear-box, and won the first race in which it was entered, a feat which caused a great deal of nail biting amongst Lotus, B.R.M., March, Ferrari,

Matra, Surtees, Brabham, McLaren, and Tyrell teams.

It took Ryan little time to discover how different the style of his work was going to be from what he'd done at Llanarch. To begin with, publicity concentrated on roadholding, performance, and durability, all subjects mentioned only reluctantly at Llanarch. Then there was the attitude of management. Instead of the stultifying hand of an organisation which actually prided itself on its unchangeability, at Drew all was change, there was a pioneering spirit as if the motor car had only just been invented, and new ideas were welcomed, discussed, and examined without prior and automatic reservations.

Stanley Drew came into Ryan's office on the third day, unannounced, on his own, and without any fuss. He was a tall, thin, bespectacled man, already balding at the forehead, who made no effort to inspire confidence and loyalty yet managed to do both. He sat on the edge of the desk and spoke about Ryan's job for less than a minute, then about their Formula One car for twenty.

Even Ryan's secretary was different. She not only was young, attractive, and given to wearing see-through blouses, she was actually intelligent.

.   .   .   .   .

On the Thursday—a sunny, balmy day which suddenly introduced spring—Ryan was called to the managing director's office, on the top floor of the five-storey administrative building. Graham Eccles was as important to Drew Motors as Stanley Drew, yet in a different and opposite way. Drew was the genius from whom all the sparks flew, Eccles was the man who sorted out the sparks and blew on the useful ones. He was large, nearly gross, dewlaps gave him the look of a bloodhound, and his manner was always easy: it was difficult to imagine any crisis severe enough to upset him.

He came round his desk, looking top heavy because his legs were short and slim. 'Nice of you to come up. I thought it would be an idea to have a general chat. . . . Grab a seat.'

Ryan sat down and found himself experiencing an immediate and instinctive liking for this man, something he very rarely knew.

Eccles spoke in general terms about Ryan's job, making it clear that Ryan was expected to use his own judgement and discretion and not to refer decisions to higher authority except in very major cases. 'That way, you make or break the job and it's your head for the chopping block or the laurel leaves. Bertie Field, your predecessor, did a wonderful job and we were all very sorry when he was so suddenly taken fatally ill. My guess is you're going to do at least as well.'

'Thanks,' replied Ryan gratefully. It was astonishing to find himself in a job which so exactly suited his temperament, especially after the nightmarish time he'd been through.

'There's one last point. We're looking to get more publicity out of our Formula One racing. Do you follow the sport?'

'Only vaguely, I'm afraid, as I know little about it.'

'Then one of your early jobs is to learn. Our trouble is, of course, that although it's become a very popular sport, the interest in it is severely restricted to initiates, mainly men—unlike football, for instance, where all of us can become excited over a world cup match—so that success starts with limited publicity appeal. So if you can work out an angle or two that will attract a wider interest, particularly female, that's what we want.' The telephone rang and Eccles answered it briefly. 'Sorry about that,' he said, as he replaced the receiver. 'I've just had a thought. The quickest way for you to become *au fait* with the racing scene is to jog along with the team to some of their races. How does that idea strike you?'

'As a first-class one.'

'Good. Well, we're not competing again until the next Nürburgring race for Formula One—it's not a *grande épreuve*—and you can travel with them.' He wrote a note on his pad. 'Keep your fingers crossed for another win. And remember one thing—never, ever, put into cold print what the racing programme costs us in spite of the sponsorship we've managed to get. We just daren't face the truth!'

.   .   .   .   .

Nina never really bothered about money—figures, she claimed, confused her—so that Ryan had little difficulty in explaining how he'd been able to afford the second-hand Morris Marina, bought with the dollars he'd been paid in New York. He murmured H.P. and said they'd easily be able to keep up the payments and knew she'd never bother to wonder how they could do this on their reduced income when they'd so many other debts to pay off.

The drive from the factory—which was surrounded by its own test track—was long but pleasant, passing as it did mainly through countryside. Ryan liked the peace of the countryside and the time-honoured anarchy of the layout of fields and hedges which made it a planner's nightmare, but it was not a strong enough liking ever to have made him think of living in it.

Beyond the countryside was East Rushton, a mixture of new housing estates, rows of deteriorating Victorian and Edwardian houses whose grounds were not big enough to make it worth while to pull them down and rebuild, some shops, and two light industrial estates which had failed to give employment to as many people as the planners had promised when seeking to overcome strong opposition to development.

On Monday he arrived home at six-thirty. As he parked the car in the garage, he thought that one day he'd buy a Drew G.T. It would fill Jack's cup of happiness to roll up in one of those when fetching him from school.

Nina met him in the hall and kissed him. 'You're looking really well, at last, Hilary.'

'That's not to be wondered at.'

'Let's go out to the films after supper? We haven't been for ages and ages.'

'That depends on which cinema. You're not, I hope, thinking of that film which is guaranteed to send every woman home in floods of tears?'

'Stop being so superior and come and have a drink.'

'A dozen drinks won't soften me against that perticular tear-jerker. I say we stay at home and watch the telly.'

'You're forgetting we haven't got one.' She looked up at him. 'Wouldn't it be an idea to get on to the rental people tomorrow morning and tell them to bring out a colour set?'

'You don't think we ought to be content with black and white for a bit?'

'But black and white's so boring.' She linked her arm with his. 'And now for a little surprise.'

'Surprise?'

'In the sitting-room.'

They went in and he saw on one of the small tables the silver ice bucket her parents had given them and in it a bottle of champagne.

She spoke a trifly shyly. 'We always have champagne on an anniversary . . . And there's plenty of time before the film starts.'

He looked puzzled. 'But what anniversary is it? It's not your birthday . . .'

'It's a week since you started the new job.'

He laughed, kissed her, and told her that as an economist she made a great cook. He took the bottle out of the ice bucket, removed the foil and wire, and edged out the cork with his thumbs.

He filled the two fluted glasses and passed one across. 'To the job,' he said, as he raised his glass, 'and may we have an anniversary every week for the next few years.'

The telephone rang an hour later, as he poured out the last of the champagne into their two glasses.

'We've another job,' said Smith.

'That's very kind of you,' he answered, 'but I won't be doing any more work for you.'

'Why not?'

'I've just landed a full-time job. Thanks very much for all the work you've given me . . .'

'Shit you!' Smith's voice was vicious.

'I'm sorry,' Ryan said, 'but now I've got this job I just simply can't do part-time work any more. In any case, that trip to New York . . .'

The connexion was cut and the croaking dialling tone began.

11

Peter Comyns had always found it difficult to make friends, although he seldom had trouble getting along with people in a casual manner. He recognised that the fault, if it could be called a fault, was his. He liked to stand back until satisfied that the other person was all he claimed to be and mostly the other person saw this hesitation as coldness. Polly Comyns was just the opposite in character. She was ruled by emotion and instinct. She often teased him about his wariness and his initial withdrawal, although she'd never told him how much she regretted his inability to give a warmer impression because then he might have risen higher in the police force: even chief superintendents wanted to believe they were liked for themselves and not their rank.

Ryan parked in front of Comyns' house. In south-west Rushton, it was semi-detached but so solidly built, in the middle thirties, that little noise came through from the other half. He pressed the front-door bell and while he waited he rehearsed yet again what he wanted to say and how he'd say it.

Polly opened the door and he went into the hall. 'Hilary—what a lovely surprise! Hasn't it been cold again at night, just when it seemed we'd really reached spring? When I can find a handsome man with a fortune I'm going to go and live with him in Tenerife where it's always warm and sunny. Do tell me, how's the new job going? I've been longing to know.'

'I'm really going to enjoy it.

'Then isn't that wonderful! Pete's in the sitting-room.' She opened the door on her right. 'Pete, it's Hilary. So trot out the drinks.'

After greeting Ryan, Comyns left the room, returning very soon with a bottle of the sherry he always served and three glasses on a well-worn wooden tray. Anderson, as tactless as always, referred to the sherry as camel's piss.

Polly talked rapidly as her husband poured out the drinks. 'Hilary says the new job is great, Pete, so isn't that wonderful! We kept thinking of you, Hilary, not being able to find a job. At least with Pete he may not be well paid, but he's not likely to be made redundant whilst the crime rate keeps rising.'

'No redundancy,' said Comyns in his dry, half-humorous, half-serious manner, 'only forcible retirement at a fixed age.'

'It's not the same thing at all. You come out with a pension and get a cracking good job with a security

81

firm and make more money than you're doing now.'

'And we live happily ever after?'

'Stop being so horribly cynical,' she retorted.

Ryan, wishing he'd been given a whisky instead of the sherry to ginger up his courage, drank quickly as he waited for a break in Polly's chatter. When it came, he said: 'Pete, I've come along for a bit of advice. Hope you don't mind?'

'Only too glad to help.' Comyns settled back in the chair and his long, thin face became virtually expressionless.

'I've a friend who lives up north and I happened to meet him the other day and saw something was worrying him so asked him what was wrong. He tried to deny anything was, but in the end told me, I suppose on the old principle that a trouble shared is a trouble halved. I told him I couldn't advise him what to do, but that I knew a friend who would.'

Comyns looked briefly at Ryan. 'Presumably, it's a criminal matter?'

'It . . . it could be.'

Comyns nodded.

'I should add it's strictly confidential.' Ryan drew heavily on his cigarette. 'Richard was like me in being made redundant in his forties, only he's now worse off because he still hasn't a job. Some weeks ago, he was rung up at home and the caller said he represented a firm who transported small items of very high security risk and would Richard like a part-time job with them? Naturally, he jumped at the chance. He found their method of work was a bit odd, but at first didn't think anything of this.'

'How odd?'

'He was told to meet someone at New Street

82

Station, Birmingham, collect a parcel and take that by train to Liverpool. In Liverpool the parcel was collected from him in Prater public library and he was paid twenty-five pounds.' Ryan looked at Comyns, but the other's face still expressed no discernible emotion. 'Twenty-five quid was a lot of money to someone in his fix, so he just forgot the oddness and hoped there'd be another job. He went to Bonn and was asked to bring back a piece of jewellery, but when it was given to him it was made pretty clear he was being asked to do a bit of smuggling for which he'd get a hundred pounds. He couldn't afford to turn down the chance. The next trip he was sent to Rome with a small parcel and on handing it over he was given over a million and a half lire—it worked out at a thousand pounds. Naturally, that put the wind up him because it was obvious he wasn't being paid for any ordinary sort of job. Now he's wondering what in the hell it was he took that last time.'

'What an extraordinary set of circumstances!' said Polly. She turned to her husband. 'Have you the slightest idea what it's all about, Pete?'

Comyns put down his glass on the small imitation pie-crust table by his side. 'Your friend Richard has been drawn into heroin smuggling.' He stubbed out his cigarette.

'Heroin!' repeated Polly, wide-eyed.

Ryan stared dully at the fire. Until now, by some further legerdemain of self-deception, he'd managed to persuade himself that the parcel he'd taken to New York had not contained some form of drugs.

'What on earth does Hilary's friend do now?' asked Polly.

Comyns, with the irritating habit of his, did not

answer for quite a time. Then he said: 'There's only one thing he possibly can do—tell the police what's happened.'

Ryan said: 'He thought of that, of course, but where does that leave him?'

'A heroin runner.'

'But if he didn't know what he was doing . . .' began Polly.

Comyns interrupted her. 'He knew from the beginning something was wrong.'

'He swears he didn't,' said Ryan.

'Then he's either a liar or a very great fool.'

'Suppose he does as you say and tells the police —what'll happen to him?'

'He'll be questioned to see how much help he can actually give towards tracing the principals and then probably he'll be charged under the Dangerous Drugs Acts.'

'Then why on earth should he risk all this and go to the police at all?'

'Because he's got himself mixed up in something bloody horrible and dangerous. By helping the police, the penalty may well be less severe than it would otherwise be.'

'If the police are going to charge him, there'll be publicity?'

'Certainly.'

'Which must affect his job?'

'I thought you said he still hasn't found one?'

He's obviously hoping to get one soon,' replied Ryan hurriedly, trying to cover his gaffe. 'Boiled down, you're saying he's in an impossible position.'

'He's only himself to blame for finding himself there.'

Polly spoke indignantly. 'Pete, you're not showing much sympathy for this man.'

'It's very difficult,' Comyns replied grimly, 'to feel
the slightest sympathy for anyone in the remotest
way connected with the drug racket.'

.   .   .   .   .

The telephone rang. Nina, at a critical point in the
intricate knitting pattern, swore as she hurriedly
tried to complete the row, then swore again when,
in her haste, she dropped a stitch. She put the knitting
on the arm of the chair.

She crossed the hall and picked up the telephone
receiver. 'Three eight three eight two.'

'Can I speak to Mr. Ryan, please.'

'I'm sorry, he's out. Who is that?'

'The name's Smith.'

She wondered who he was because his voice held
a crude, and she thought cruel, timbre to it. 'He
should be back at any moment now. Would you like
to ring a bit later on or shall I get him to ring you?'

'I'll do the honours, Mrs. Ryan. Thanks for your
help.'

After replacing the receiver, she thought about the
call. It worried her, but she couldn't be certain why.
Then she wondered if it was because the man had
sounded, just before he rang off, as if he had been
silently laughing?

.   .   .   .   .

Comyns accompanied Ryan out of the house and over
to the Marina which was parked in the short drive

to the garage. 'Is this you new car, Hilary? I must say I'm disappointed. I expected you to be racing around in a Drew G.T., burning up the roads and breaking all the traffic laws.'

Ryan laughed. 'As a matter of fact, I've promised myself one when we've got ourselves straight financially. I'll be given the chance of having one cheaply from the test fleet—provided any survive the succession of heavy-footed motoring journalists.'

'Promise me a spin in it?'

'That's a date. And many thanks for all your help.'

'Hilary, hammer home the message to your friend —he's no options left. He must go to the police if he's to avoid much worse trouble later on.'

'I'll tell him that.'

On his three-mile drive home, Ryan's thoughts were bitterly rebellious. Why couldn't Comyns have shown sympathy and understanding, been less the frigid police officer, more the friend? How could anyone go to the police and tell them everything if the only result was to be accused of drug smuggling? And why had Comyns so righteously assumed a guilty knowledge of the contents of the last parcel?

The Marina's headlights picked out the wooden gates of his drive and he turned in. The garage was open and he parked inside, then edged his way out between the brick wall and the car. He swung the heavy wooden doors shut and made certain the lock clicked.

'Mr. Ryan?'

He was startled by the voice because he had heard no approaching footsteps. He turned. Two men, large, their faces for some reason featureless despite the scattered street light which filtered through the ornamental cherry trees. 'Yes. What do you . . . ?'

The blow landed in his stomach with such force that he immediately doubled up, pain exploding through his body. As he retched, his hair was grabbed and he was wrenched upright. Something bag-like was jerked over his head.

He was hurried along the ground with most of his weight taken by his assailants. Shocked and bewildered, his stomach a sheet of fire, close to vomiting, he made an effort to call for help. Immediately, fingers dug into his throat and flattened his windpipe. Incredibly, within seconds the agony of his pumping lungs became so great that he forgot all other pain.

He was bundled, so callously that both his ankles and hip were badly bruised, into something he identified as a car. The engine started. He tried to move out of the doubled-up position in which he was because cramp was already spreading through his right leg and a shoe crashed into his side to tell him to be still.

After a time he was quite unable to judge, in acute discomfort because the hood made it difficult to breathe and the stuffy heat bathed his face in perspiration, the car stopped. The hood was pulled off his head. He gulped down the fresh air and was just able to make out that there were three men in the car —one on either side of him and the driver. Outside it was dark, though in the sky was the glow of the lights of Rushton.

He was dragged out of the car, his right arm wrenched round his back and held at the point of pain to prevent any attempt at escape. One man, a dark shadow, stood immediately in front of him. He opened his mouth to speak, but was hit violently in the stomach. His right arm was released and he collapsed to the ground. He vomited, explosively.

In time, the mists of agony receded. He heard the order, which seemed to come from far away, to get up. Slowly, he dragged himself to a crouching position and then stood.

He was hit again in the stomach. As he lay squirming on the ground, he again vomited with a violence so great it seemed he must be dying from ruptured intestines.

Gradually, he became aware of the stench and he weakly came to his knees and tried to clean his face and clothes with a handkerchief.

'Get up.'

He stood up, utterly terrified they would hit him again: turned into a coward by three blows.

'Listen to this, mug.'

There was a slight metallic click, then voices, tinny in tone, began to speak. 'You'd be Mr. Ryan—right?' 'Yes, that's right.' 'So where d'you live?' 'In England.' 'Man, you surprise me!' 'What I mean is . . .' 'What's the name of your house, Mr. Ryan?' 'Thorndale House. But what does that matter?' 'And the street and town?' 'Gerard Street, in Rushton. But surely . . . ?' 'Just checking. Have you brought over anything from London?' 'I've a small parcel for you.' 'Then give, man.' 'So now, Mr. Ryan, you'd like what's yours? Enjoy your films, man. They say they're great.'

'Recognise that?'

'Yes,' he answered hoarsely.

'While this was being recorded, you were being

shot on super fast sixteen-mill film. The New York narcotics squad would be real interested in the film and tape. Right?'

The stench made him suddenly retch, but this time he did not actually vomit. Despite all the pain, his mind was filled with revulsion at his degraded state.

'So listen, mug, when we tell you to travel, you travel.'

For some ridiculous reason, he imagined he could reason with them. 'But I can't any more as I've a job. I'll have to travel for them when I'm told to.'

'Doing what?'

'With the Drew racing team. You must understand I didn't know what was in that parcel . . .'

'Belt up.'

He shut up. Slowly and painfully, he tried to clean himself up further.

'You've got a wife,' said the man in his hoarse, crude voice. 'How'd she like a gutful of what you've just had?'

'Oh, Christ!' Ryan mumbled.

'We'll be in touch.'

They jammed the hood back over his head and bundled him into the car. Under the hood, the stench became even worse than it had been before and he vomited yet again, to add to his misery.

The car stopped and he was roughly pitched out, tripping over his feet to collapse on to the ground. They'd left the hood on and by the time he'd clawed this off the car was out of sight.

In a way he was shocked to see his house unchanged, as if he believed he could not suffer so much in isolation. He stumbled up to the front door, fumbled in his coat pocket for the key and found it, opened the door.

'You've been a long time, Hilary,' Nina called out from the sitting-room. 'I was beginning to get a little worried.' She walked into the hall and did not immediately look at him but at the grandfather clock. 'There was a telephone call for you . . .' She had turned and her expression became frozen from shock and her soft brown eyes filled with terror. 'My God, what's happened?'

12

Dr. Enton was middle-aged and he had an abrupt way that those who looked for a bedside manner found rude, a presbyterian's dislike of malingerers and moaners, and an endless, comforting patience when dealing with real illness. He straightened up from the bed. 'O.K. You can button up.'

Ryan buttoned up his pyjama jacket and pulled up the trousers. Nina carefully tucked the bed-clothes back over him.

'I can't find any traces of serious injury,' said the doctor, 'but contact me immediately at the first signs of any internal bleeding or if there's any pain more specific than the ones your husband's mentioned.'

Nina nodded. Inclined to be fussed by small

troubles, she had the inner strength to meet really serious trouble with great courage and practical ability.

'You can put the ointment on as often as you like and it will help to take out some of the bruising. And I repeat, don't hesitate to call me whatever the time.'

'I'll do that. And thanks very much for coming out.'

Enton shut his brown leather suitcase in which he carried his equipment. He spoke to Ryan. 'Don't try to belittle the injuries and rush around the place before you're fit, just to show what a fine strapping man you really are. You've suffered some pretty nasty bruising.'

'I'll not be attempting the three-minute mile for a couple of days,' said Ryan.

'You must have fallen very heavily and clumsily?'

'Yes, I did.'

Enton looked hard at Ryan, then he spoke to Nina. 'Very well,' he said briskly, making it plain he'd pry no further. 'I'll be along again tomorrow morning.'

Ryan said good night and when they'd left he relaxed completely and closed his eyes. The pain in his stomach was still thick, but his face was clean and all he could smell was eau-de-Cologne.

Nina returned to the bedroom, sat down on the bed, and reached under the sheet for his hand which she held tightly. 'You've got to tell the police,' she said.

'No.'

'But in God's name, why not? Those terrible men could have killed you.'

He shook his head. 'They knew exactly how far to go.' He suddenly coughed and his face screwed up to the sharp pain.

'Why did they do it?'

'Because I'd refused to carry on working for them.'

'But that's so . . . so senseless. Are they animals?'

It was as good a description as any, he thought.

'If you don't tell the police, this could happen again.'

'No. They've made their point and now it's all over and done with.'

Her tone became frantic. 'Hilary, you're not telling me the truth. Please, why won't you go to the police?'

'I told you, if I do the story of my part will come out.'

'But how could you really be blamed if you didn't know it was heroin?'

'I didn't know only because I refused to. Any sensible man allowing himself to think would have realised it was something vicious.'

'Are . . . are you sure the men won't ever come back?'

'Quite sure.'

She let go of his hand and stood up. 'It was utterly horrible seeing you in the hall.'

She left to go to the bathroom. On returning, she undressed and just before she slipped her nightdress over her head he imagined brutal fists thudding into her slack-fleshed stomach.

After she'd put out the light, kissed him good night and fondled his cheek in a gesture of reassurance, she turned over to fall asleep almost immediately, emotionally exhausted. He stared up at the vaguely outlined ceiling. At all costs, he had to protect her from being attacked.

.   .   .   .   .

Walking only slightly stiffly, Ryan crossed from the administration building to the racing division. The wind was light and there were not many clouds around so that the day had all the warm charm of real spring.

The racing department used three buildings, huddled together by the north bend of the test track, which had been there when Drew Motors bought the site. Built of yellow bricks and with dirt-stained asbestos roofing, they hardly epitomised from the outside the glamour of Formula One racing. In front of the middle shed, looking brutal in lines, was a blood-red Ferrari 365GTC4.

Inside, three mechanics were working on two cars, fitting the latest series Cosworth engine to one and adjusting the rear brake calipers of the other. Beyond, stacked against the wall, were four piles of racing tyres and wheels—two sets of slicks and two sets of wet weather—a third monocoque chassis bare of any attachments and seemingly little resembling a racing car, and a complete rear axle and gear-box assembly.

Ryan greeted the mechanics. They were all relatively young, all dedicated, and the hours they worked would have given apoplexy to the men on the production lines in the factory. The red-headed, cheerful Willink told him Hugh was in the office along with Steve Barenwell. Obviously, he thought, the Ferrari was Barenwell's.

93

The three buildings were all interconnected and the offices were in the left-hand one, reached either from the outside or through the assembly shed. He went through. Hugh Clyne, the team manager and head of the department, sat behind his littered desk, and Barenwell, wearing a suit that had clearly been made in Savile Row, sat on one corner of it.

Clyne introduced Ryan. Barenwell, tall, thin, sardonic-faced, and with a slight stutter at times, shook hands, called him Hilary with the easy familiarity of the entertainment world, said he was looking forward to a mass of publicity when they won at the Ring, then looked at his many-dialled watch and left. Even in that short time, Ryan was intrigued by the strong personality of a man who had been famous for several years though he'd never been in the really exclusive top flight of drivers: there was arrogance, bounding self-confidence, a hint of contempt for anyone who lived a normal life, and yet an easy, friendly attitude which suggested he wasn't such a bastard when one got to know him.

Clyne settled back in the chair and belched. 'Steve's confident we'll stand up to the hammering of the Ring, but I don't know . . .' He shook his head. 'The only time I believe a car's really going to last is when I see it finishing without the driver pushing it over the line.' He grinned. 'Not that the pampered drivers of today would ever do anything so energetic as push!'

'What exactly is so special about the Nürburgring?' asked Ryan, as he sat down in front of the desk. 'I'd better get to know something about it if I'm to try to milk some publicity from the race.'

Clyne clasped his pudgy hands behind his back.

'It's recently been vastly improved at the cost of untold millions of marks, but it's still the same old Ring at heart: just over fourteen miles of chassis-wrenching track and a hundred and seventy-one corners that can be guaranteed to prove wrong every suspension that's ever been built. But to try to describe it further than that . . .' He lowered his hands. 'I know. I'll get Steve to run you round the track when we're over there.' He roared with laughter. 'Then you'll be able to write volumes—if you survive.'

'I don't know I want to trouble Barenwell so close to a race.'

'It won't.' Clyne's round, baggy face became thoughtful. 'It's odd. Steve still laps up the praise— tell him he's a ruddy marvel behind a wheel and you've made his day. You'd have thought by now he wouldn't need to be told he's good, wouldn't you? Maybe it's like the millionaire who chuckles with glee when he saves himself a quid with some petty bit of meanness. Have you discovered that about millionaires, Hilary?'

Ryan had become reasonably used to Clyne's habit of changing the subject under discussion. 'The only rich person I know is a bit of a bastard from every direction.'

After a brief discussion, he said: 'I've come for the griff on our trip to Germany.'

Clyne searched amongst the clutter on his desk and finally picked up a roneod sheet which he passed across. 'Here's the itinerary. We're staying in Daun because I don't like big hotels and I do like draught Moselle, but Steve'll be stopping somewhere smart because that's the way he always wants it. We're motoring over, independent of the transporter, on

95

the Wednesday. Is that O.K. by you?'

'Fine.' Ryan folded up the paper and put it in his wallet. He stood up.

'You wouldn't have any pull at Cosworths, would you?' asked Clyne.

'Not an ounce. Why?'

'I keep needling them for one of their special engines for Steve and they keep telling me the story that all their engines give the same power. If Jon France's Lotus hasn't been pulling extra revs, I'll retire and grow gooseberries.'

Ryan left the office and returned through the assembly area. The engine had been fitted to the nearer chassis and the back-axle assembly was being bolted on to it. Even without the wheels, the Drew looked exactly what it was—a desperately dangerous projectile.

.   .   .   .   .

During supper, the main dish of which was Nina's adaptation of a coquilles St.-Jacques, Ryan said: 'We leave early on the Wednesday for Germany and all being well will come back on Monday evening.'

'That'll make a nice break for you,' she said.

He looked quickly at her. Now when they spoke to each other they seemed to spend most of their time guarding their tongues and keeping to neutral topics. Each knew the other's mind must be filled with fear, but each of them, ostrich-like, believed that if he or she said nothing critical the other might forget to be afraid. 'I went along to the racing department after lunch and met Steve Barenwell for the first time.'

'Who?'

'Steve Barenwell, the driver. You must have heard of him. I thought you women all went kinky crazy over he-men who risk their lives like that?'

She smiled briefly. 'At my age?'

'Didn't you tell me once when you were young you heard it's never too late? He's handsome, dashing, heroic, and a bit vicious.'

'And one day he'll probably kill himself and the women in his life will be left with nothing but tears.' She spoke with sudden bitterness.

Somehow, their conversation had twisted round into dangerous waters. 'Nina . . . Stop thinking all the time that the worst is going to happen.'

She searched his face. 'Hilary, d'you swear you're keeping nothing from me?'

'Haven't I done so again and again? Why won't you believe me?'

'Because there's a shadow in your eyes.'

'You're imagining things.' He picked up the bottle of Valpolicella. 'Have another glassful and forget shadows.'

'No, thanks.' She watched him refill his own glass. 'Hilary, remember how we decided to cut back on our drink—yet you've been drinking a lot recently.'

He spoke almost angrily. 'Are you saying I'm turning into an old soak?' The moment he'd spoken, he regretted his words because her soft brown eyes filled with distress and her mouth worked. 'I'm sorry,' he muttered contritely.

'Can't you see that I don't care how much you drink so long . . . So long as it's not because really you're scared.'

'Console yourself with the thought that I'm drink-

ing heavily because my great-grandfather was a dip-
somaniac and I've always wanted to follow in his
footsteps.'

She looked uncertainly at him, then finally smiled.
'That's all right, then. All I've got to do is wait until
you get cirrhosis of the liver and inherit everything.'

'Especially the debts.'

The front doorbell rang and immediately her eyes
were filled with a flood of terror. He spoke softly.
'It's only someone perfectly respectable and harmless.'

In fact, it was Comyns and a man he introduced
initially simply as Mr. Foxley. Comyns apologised
for disturbing them, but said he'd like a chat on an
important matter. Nina, apparently noticing no
extra stiffness in Comyn's manner, said she'd get
some coffee while they went into the sitting-room.

Comyns spoke very abruptly as he sat down on
the settee. 'Mr. Foxley is a detective superintendent
from county H.Q.'

Surprised, but as yet nothing more, Ryan studied
Foxley more closely. He saw a well-built man in
middle age with unusually broad shoulders, a square
face, friendly eyes topped by luxuriant eyebrows,
ruddy complexion, and a chin which was square and
uncompromising. He wore a suit that had become
baggy, yet which thereby seemed to suit his bluff
personality.

'Mr. Ryan, I believe you've a friend who's got himself into a load of trouble?' said Foxley.

'Who told you that?' In the circumstances it was a
ridiculous question, but shocked surprise jerked the
words out of Ryan.

'Mr. Comyns,' answered Foxley gravely, as if

98

there might have been some doubt on that score.

Ryan faced Comyns. 'I spoke to you in the strictest confidence.'

Comyns made no answer, but his pale blue eyes seemed to become a shade bleaker.

'You'd no right to tell anyone else.'

Foxley spoke, in his slow measured voice. 'He had a duty to tell me, Mr. Ryan, as his senior officer.'

Ryan stared at Comyns. Their friendship stretched back almost to when Nina and he had married and had first lived into Thorndale House and in that time he'd come to know Comyns as a bit of a queer stick who lived by the rule book and was inflexible in thought and action, yet who had the inestimable virtue of being a true friend. Yet Comyns had betrayed that friendship apparently as easily as another man would down a pint of beer.

Foxley had been watching Ryan's face. 'A man can have several loyalties and be forced to choose which to honour.'

'And get his choice hopelessly bloody wrong.' Ryan was slowly beginning to experience to the full the bitterness of betrayal.

'I'm afraid that depends on your viewpoint. When it comes to drug smuggling, Mr. Ryan, every member of the force can have only one.' Foxley hadn't changed the even tone of his voice, yet now it contained a hint of sharpness. Anyone fooled by his original slow and pleasant manner would now have had sharply to revise his judgement of the other's real character. 'Will you tell me something? Do you, in fact, have a friend called Richard or were you describing events that have happened to you?'

'To me?' Ryan tried to sound amazed.

99

Foxley waited.

The silence continued. 'You don't think I'd have got mixed up in a thing like that, do you?' demanded Ryan, no longer able to keep quiet.

'Your story has to be wrong because you said Richard had been sent to Rome with a parcel. The route of drugs out of England is to America, not Italy. The fact that a thousand pounds was paid for the journey shows it has to be drugs that were carried.'

Ryan, very conscious of a dried-out mouth, lit a cigarette.

'You've recently been to New York,' said Foxley.

'No,' denied Ryan automatically and clumsily, and then he remembered how Nina had told Polly he was going and Polly had laughingly wished he'd take her for a dirty weekend as she'd always wanted to go there.

'Perhaps,' said Foxley, in avuncular tones, 'it'll help you to make up your mind to be frank to learn a bit about the drug scene.' He waited, but when there was no answer, continued. 'The producers, the poppy growers, are in the Near and Far East and the consumers, the addicts, are mainly in America, but with a growing number in this and other European countries. The logistical problem is to get the opium turned into heroin and the heroin delivered to the consumer, despite the efforts of the police forces of many nations.' He spoke casually and in terms that could have applied to ordinary products, but there was something about the set of his mouth which said that he only did this to disguise his true feelings.

He reminded Ryan of the old history master at school: pleasant, talking in simple terms so that he

100

could be certain his rather dim audience would understand, but with something heavy at hand in case of unruliness or inattention.

'There are three main poppy-growing areas: Turkey, a large triangle in Burma between China, Laos, and Thailand, and China. Turkey is supposed to be stopping production, mainly due to American pressure, but I'll believe that when it happens. In any case, the Chinese, believing it to be in their interests to encourage drug addiction in the Western world, will merely step up production to make up the loss. The opium is shipped down to laboratories —Hong Kong is very popular because close to water the odour of the drug disperses more quickly—and chemically turned into morphine. The morphine is shipped to other laboratories—far more complex— and turned into heroin. Many of these latter laboratories are in Italy or the southern coast of France, around Marseilles. Once it's become heroin, of course, it's worth thousands of times what it was as opium, even to the manufacturers.

'The most profitable market is the United States. Therefore the main lines of transport lie from France and Italy to the States, although seldom directly.

'Twenty years ago, the trade was fragmented and not very highly organised and there were transportation troubles, losses, double-crossings. There was a meeting in which the American bosses studied the problems and out of this and other studies came a rationalisation of the system.' Again, he spoke in ordinary commercial terms, but with a twist to his mouth.

'It was agreed that from then on the heroin would

101

be brought from the manufacturers at the place of manufacture, leaving the Americans responsible for shipping it to the States. As runners, really dependable men were employed who had no record in narcotics. Unfortunately for the mobs, though, these men were, like all criminals, predictable and very reluctant to change any system that had proved itself by working. In time the narcotics squads of various nations got to identify them. There was full co-operation between police of several nationalities, a concentrated clean-up, a lot of heroin was flushed, and most of the best runners were imprisoned.

'The American bosses always learn from experience. It was obvious that the direct chain through to them had been and always would be dangerous, leading to identification of runners, so they had to split the chain. They did this by employing middlemen, who were paid very highly to pick up heroin from the manufacturers and deliver it to their organisations in the States.

'The English middlemen have—unfortunately—shown themselves to be men of imagination. Obviously, if they used their own villains as runners, identification by the police would be an eventual certainty—as it was with the Americans. So they hit on a very ingenious system which ensured their anonymity and in the event of failure limited their losses. You know the rest, don't you?'

'No,' muttered Ryan.

Foxley sighed. 'They search for men whose background places them above suspicion, but whose honesty has been undermined by circumstances, men of executive background, used to a very comfortable life, suddenly made redundant and finding their comfortable life threatened. Their names are usually obtained quite legitimately, from employment agencies.

'Their method of selection shows a great deal of cunning: it follows the course of a confidence trickster who's successful only when he finds a victim who, consciously or unconsciously, is willing to take advantage of another if apparently to the benefit of himself.

'The redundant executive is, by definition, very hard up and probably terrified that his world as he'd always known it has come to an end: his past way of life usually ensures he's soon badly in debt after his salary ceases, despite any top-hat payments. He's offered a part-time job in somewhat strange circumstances. After it, he's paid just enough to make him wonder what in the hell's going on . . . This, Mr. Ryan, is the moment of truth, isn't it?'

Ryan lit another cigarette.

'The totally honest man will recognise that no wholly reputable firm would begin to operate in the way in which this one does. But the man who is not totally honest or whose honesty has been badly bruised by his fear of poverty will find ways of persuading himself that really everything is quite O.K., even if unusual.'

Ryan remembered Nina's fear and how he'd deceived himself into stilling all his doubts.

'A second job is offered. The honest man says to hell with it and there's the end. The slightly dishonest man accepts the second job. Now, it's made clear to him that he's being asked to do something just a little bit illegal. Smuggling something quite innocuous, perhaps. If the victim doesn't take fright but shows some hesitation, he's told the pay is quite a bit higher than last time. Some men will drop out despite this, others will accept and somehow continue to talk their consciences into silence.

'If the victim delivers the smuggled object as directed, then he's hooked. He's given a third job and this time it's either to bring a parcel from Italy or southern France into England, or to take one from England to the States—the indirect route to the States is always taken because the direct routes are subject to greater narcotic surveillance. That parcel contains heroin. On handing it over, he's photographed and then if he ever tries to cause trouble he can, if still potentially of use, be blackmailed into continuing work. Should he ever be caught, he'll confess everything, of course, but his evidence won't be worth a spit in the dark because all he can give are descriptions of the few contacts he's had and his descriptions will be virtually valueless because none of the contacts will be known by the police to be in the drug racket.

'Are you interested in how we know so much about their methods?'

Ryan didn't answer.

'One of their runners tried to double-cross them: we found him just before he died.' Foxley leaned forward and dropped his voice: he spoke earnestly. 'Mr. Ryan, because you've had a lot of bad luck you've acted stupidly, but now you've just got to face facts. We've come to help you do that.'

So strong was the air of sympathic understanding, so attuned was it to his instinctive desire for absolution by confession, that he was about to tell them everything when Comyns was suddenly seized by a fit of coughing. Ryan looked at him and immediately remembered his gross act of betrayal. 'None of that concerns me.'

If Foxley was disappointed, he didn't show it. He remained quiet, courteous, and blandly confident. 'Come now—we've checked your bank accounts and know you've drawn no large sums of money recently, yet you've settled several of your outstanding accounts with local traders and have paid for your car with cash.'

Ryan was shocked to discover his life could have been so closely investigated without his learning a thing about this.

'We know so much, you might as well just tell us the rest,' said Foxley.

Again, Ryan was almost tempted into confessing, but then he remembered the men who had so savagely beaten him up. 'It's all double Dutch to me.'

Nina came into the room with the coffee on a tray. She put the tray down by Ryan's chair. 'I'm not having any, Hilary, because I thought you'd rather carry on without me.' There was a slight query in her voice, as if she were asking him whether he really would. Then she noticed his expression for the first time and drew in her breath sharply. 'What . . .' She turned. 'Pete, what are you doing here?' Her voice was suddenly shrill.

Comyns brushed his moustache. 'We just want a chat with Hilary.' He showed a trace of uneasiness, as if his granite-like sense of duty had for the first time suffered a small crack.

'What d'you want to talk to him about?'

'It's all O.K.,' said Ryan.

She slowly walked past Foxley, who'd stood up as she entered, across to the door. As she stared at Ryan

105

her eyes openly expressed fright and unwittingly she made it obvious she knew her husband had cause to be afraid of the police. She left.

Foxley sat down. Ryan poured out the coffee and handed the tray around, automatically observing all the social customs even at such a time.

Foxley stirred sugar into his coffee. 'I suppose you realise you could be arrested now for smuggling heroin into the States?'

'If . . . if it had been at all like you're suggesting, I wouldn't have known what I was doing until too late.'

'The criminal intent was there: you were prepared to smuggle into the States. The fact you chose not to know it was heroin can't be any sort of defence.'

'It happened to Richard, not to me.'

Foxley drank some coffee. 'Mr. Ryan, we know how they've been working it, but until now we've never been able to identify a runner until too late. So help us and you may find the law can be merciful.'

'Are you saying there wouldn't be a trial?'

'There will have to be a trial, either here or in the States. But if we have your co-operation, we can tell the court about it and this must count in your favour.'

'I've done nothing.'

Foxley momentarily looked impatient. 'Don't you yet realise the facts? If we arrest you, there'll be publicity: if there's publicity, the mob will release evidence of your guilt as a warning to other runners not to be so clumsy as to be caught. Then, with us not saying anything in your favour, you must be seriously punished, even if it is your first offence.'

'You're trying to blackmail me into helping you,' said Ryan hoarsely. 'Just like they did . . . to Richard.

Only you're meant to be the law.'

'All I've tried to do is indicate your only feasible course of action.' Foxley checked his empty coffee cup was safe, then stood up. He sounded a little upset at the ingratitude he was being shown.

As Comyns stood up, his jerky movements expressing his uneasiness, Foxley said: 'Probably the best thing is for us to leave you to think it over and then when you realise we're right we can have another chat.' His voice carried the conviction of certainty.

Just before he and Foxley left, Comyns cleared his throat loudly and was obviously about to say something. Then he brushed his moustache, nodded, and left. Foxley politely asked Ryan to thank Mrs. Ryan for the coffee before following.

Nina came into the hall from the kitchen as Ryan turned away from the closed door. 'They know, don't they?' she demanded. 'Thank God! And you told them about that terrible beating?'

He hesitated a shade too long.

'Hilary, didn't you tell them?' She came close to him. 'Why?' Then she realised what the truth must be: that attack had been a warning for the future. She gripped him tightly. 'What are you going to do?' she whispered.

He shook his head. He didn't know.

13

Madge Jepson sat by the side of Ryan's desk and held the dictation pad on her crossed knee. 'I'm ready.'

Ryan re-read the handwritten letter, six pages long, on which Graham Eccles had scrawled: 'This could be useful?' The writer of the letter had hired the track at Monza for some enormous sum of lire and had attacked the twelve-hour record for unmodified 2000 c.c. cars, beating it by 21·4 m.p.h. So the 1937 record—until then intact through complete obscurity—had finally fallen. Would anyone really buy a Drew because of this? It had to be assumed the answer was 'Yes' or people might argue there really was no need for publicity.

'Recently at Monza, the world-famous race-track in a private park just north of Milan, an unsponsored driver decided to try to beat a record which has stood for many years despite every attempt to beat it. His choice of car was a Drew G.T. because of its built-in dependability, its magnificent roadholding, and its performance, all of which could be used to their full for twelve tortuous hours with only the few permitted alterations from standard—mainly to do with the problems of oil cooling over so long a maximum speed blind.' So far, not too many lies. 'Long-distance racing is one of the finest tests of any car. . . .'

He knew he was stringing cliché together with cliché, but those were what people readily under-

108

stood in an age of mass communication. His mind wandered. What in God's name to do: how to avoid the unavoidable? How had he ever believed the world a place of law and order, the police essentially kind towards those they were paid to protect? Detective Superintendent Foxley was smooth and friendly and as dangerous as a rattlesnake. Comyns was an upright man of honour who'd betrayed his friend. The men who'd beaten him up had used violence with a casual skill that spoke of constant practice.

He resumed dictating. 'The Drew G.T. suffered no mechanical mishap whatsoever, not even a single puncture, vivid proof for the ordinary motorist . . .'

This was terrible! He'd have to rewrite the whole damn thing. He never had been able to work well when grabbed by trouble. Foxley was going to demand a decision: co-operate or be arrested. To co-operate meant bucking the men who'd threatened Nina.

The telephone rang. Accounts wanted to know his social security number.

He finished dictating and said: 'Type that out double spacing, will you, please. It'll need a lot of pruning and rewriting.'

He watched her leave. She had a very earthy body and no doubt kept her current boy friend happy.

He doodled with a pencil. The telephone rang again. Hugh Clyne said the time of departure from Dover had been altered and he made a note of the new time and went back to his doodling and soon saw he'd fashioned a hangman's noose. The telephone rang again and this time it was the call he'd been dreading.

Foxley spoke in such a casual voice that it really

did seem as if he didn't care which course of action Ryan had decided to take. 'I must have your decision, Mr. Ryan.'

His mind frantically sought a last-second way of escape out of a situation in which he knew there could be none.

'Which is it to be?'

When a man was faced by two alternative disasters, in the final event he inevitably tried to avoid whichever was the more imminent even if such avoidance must mean incurring the other. 'I'll . . . I'll tell you what I can.' said Ryan hoarsely.

'You're very wise. At what time do you normally eat?'

'Around one o'clock.'

'I'll park outside the main factory gates at that time and we'll have a snack lunch at a pub.'

.   .   .   .   .

Foxley drove his five-year-old Triumph 2000 skilfully, but with a sharpness that betrayed to an observant onlooker something of his true nature. Twice he overtook when it was just safe, but a really prudent motorist would not have done so and in the car park of the large public house he had no compunction in stealing the space a woman in a Fiat was obviously making for.

The saloon bar was large and warm, well lit, with a number of tables and chairs, two one-armed bandits, and a collection of place-name stickers on the wall. Foxley bought ham sandwiches and two pints of bitter.

Ryan spoke. 'There's one thing got to be fixed.'

110

'What's that?'

'Nina must be protected.'

Foxley drank some beer. 'They've threatened you both, then? And now you're feeling bloody frightened because you think that by telling us the truth you may be risking her safety? Forget it. We'll protect both your wife and you.' He spoke with complete confidence as he took a battered cigarette case from his pocket and offered it. Ryan lit a cigarette and dragged the smoke down deep into his lungs.

'Tell me everything that's happened, in the order it's happened,' directed Foxley, 'and get as detailed as possible. Did the accent of anyone you spoke to suggest a district, how were the people you met dressed, did you learn anything to suggest whether they'd travelled far to meet you, what were your exact orders?'

Ryan, speaking slowly, described all that had happened. By the time he'd finished both their glasses were empty and he took them across to the bar for a refill. The plump, jovial landlord said the weather wasn't bad, was it?, but his sister was out in Tunisia and there it was like midsummer. Ryan paid and took the glasses back to the table.

After drinking, Foxley wiped some froth from his mouth with the back of his hand. 'You know,' he said, 'it's ten to one they'll use you to smuggle into this country because with your new job that's a natural.' He looked across.

Ryan waited.

'I told you that the stuff isn't taken direct from manufacturer to the States because aircraft on such flights, and ships, are so closely watched? It's moved in two, even three, stages, leaving France and Italy

111

along the most inconspicuous routes available at the time. If you're going to various parts of the Continent, they'll ship the stuff up to you by road—which allows little chance of discovery—and your task will be to get it into this country. Some may stay here, but most will be transhipped to the States by another runner.'

'If you know all this then the obvious route for them surely becomes the one to take because you'll be concentrating on the less obvious ones.'

Foxley smiled briefly. 'Quite. But if you're the villains you don't know how much we know.' He took a small card, printed and rather grubby, from his wallet. 'Here's my telephone number. Get in touch the moment you hear from them.'

Ryan took the card.

14

Ryan climbed into the passenger seat of the Ferrari and settled down in it, fixed the safety straps. Barenwell, in racing overalls but not wearing a helmet, his long black hair neatly swept back, climbed in behind the wheel. 'All set then?'

'All set,' replied Ryan.

'There's no need to look so scared, man, you can only die once!' Barenwell roared with laughter.

Ryan, staring along the vast blood-red bonnet, consoled himself with the thought that although the fact was never publicised, Barenwell suffered numerous obsessive superstitions and never dared race without half a dozen private propitiatory gestures towards the fates he publicly scorned.

Barenwell started the engine. To Ryan, it sounded quietly powerful but controllable, unlike the Formula One engines which always seemed to have gone wild and about to rev themselves apart. They drove past lock-up garages in which mechanics were preparing cars for the first practice and out of the paddock under the tunnel which brought them out on the centre of the track by the petrol pumps, the Mercedes Tower, and the pits. An official waved the Ferrari down, but after a few breezy words from Barenwell let them continue. Ryan stared at the enormous grandstand on the opposite side of the track and at the people in it and wondered where to hide the package? It seemed ridiculous to go to all the trouble of hiding it when he then told the police where it was, but those were the orders: everything had to be exactly as it would have been had he really been smuggling.

They reached the end of the pits and the Armco barrier and Ryan caught the woolfish grin on Barenwell's face and foresaw what was to happen just before it did. Barenwell stamped on the accelerator, the engine note suddenly ceased to sound controllable, and the Ferrari accelerated forward with a violence that pinned Ryan to the seat.

The first right-hander with slightly banked curve was dead ahead. They were catapulted towards it and already the scenery was a blur and the cockpit was filled with mayhem. He saw no chance of avoiding an appalling accident.

Barenwell juggled accelerator and wheel to take them round at a speed which completely terrified Ryan, not least because his senses said it was impossible. 'In a race,' shouted Barenwell, as he flicked on slight opposite lock and then straightened up, 'we take that in third at nine thousand five hundred revs.'

Ryan looked at the speedometer. It showed close to a hundred m.p.h. and still they were accelerating towards the next corner, the left-handed North Curve, even though they were almost on it. Then Barenwell stood on the brakes and the Ferrari seemed to run into an iron fist so that the whole car vibrated furiously. With heel-and-toe braking and gear changing, he flicked down through the gears with a skill that was obvious even to someone now concerned only with the chances of staying alive. 'We brake from a hundred and fifty,' shouted Barenwell.

As they went into the North Curve, the car drifted. Ryan closed his eyes. They took off over the bridge and when they landed his teeth slammed together because his mouth had been slightly open. Through the downhill section, between pine trees, Barenwell appeared to go mad, changing up and down, accelerating, flinging the car round curves and working at the wheel all the time.

'A hundred and forty in fourth,' he shouted.

They stormed round Flugplatz and down to Schwedenkreuz and flung themselves at the tight right-handed Aremberg, where some onlookers waved at them. By now, Ryan was feeling sick and he hated Barenwell for proving to him how much of a coward he could be: there was no thrill in this sort of speed, only bowel-gripping terror.

Under the Postrasse Bridge and the Ferrari doing a hundred and thirty so that the road became narrowed by speed until Ryan knew for certain this was where they finally met disaster. More violent braking, more maniacal cornering which hurled him tight against the safety belt, more wild accelerating that threw the car towards the next blurred corner.

Fifty round the Karussell and Barenwell shouting about eighty in second, the car pounding with vibration on the short, steep bank, the mirror flickering with distorted images, the wheel continuously on the move as he held them tightly in before paying off as the bank disappeared.

Little Karussell and the straight. Feeling the tail lighten dangerously as they went over each of the many crests that disturbed this long straight. Round Antoniusbuche at scarcely slackened speed and travelling parallel to the public road, rocketing past cars going in the same direction. Then, as if making one last effort to break Ryan's nerve once and for all, Barenwell took them right up to the limit for the chicane, lost it, brilliantly regained it by the use of accelerator and wheel and took them out past the Dunlop Tower, totally careless of the fact that disaster had stuck one foot into the car.

Clyne, his round face smiling broadly, behind him two mechanics in their Firestone overalls equally amused, said. 'Feel like trying a drive for the team?'

Ryan undid the safety strap and slowly climbed out of the car, conscious his legs were trembling. He leaned against the roof. A Lotus was started up and the mechanic blipped the engine, using a spanner on the throttle linkage: the sound rocked through his head. In a way he couldn't quite understand, he had experienced the violence of the speed as an extension of the violence he had suffered.

'Are you all right?' demanded Clyne, suddenly worried.

'Sure.' He jerked himself upright and saw the look of contemptuous amusement on Barenwell's face. 'I was just thinking what a pity it was we didn't have a really fast car to go round in.'

.   .   .   .   .

On Friday, on his second short practice lap round the South Curve, up the brief straight, and turning off the North Curve, the Drew dropped a valve and the mechanics had to change the engine. By the time that two and a half-hour job was completed, the Formula One practice session was over and the track was flooded with buzzing Formula V cars.

On Saturday, after continuing trouble with bottoming on some of the more notorious sections, Barenwell got down to 7 23 to be placed amongst the middle runners, then came into the pits and asked for a little less pressure in the front tyres and further adjustments to ride height. With only half an hour of practice left, the mechanics worked smartly. When Barenwell drew out of the pit, wheels just beginning to spin, he was totally careless of two photographers who stood in the pit lane and they had hastily to jump aside to avoid being hit. The note of the car rose, momentarily dipped at the gear change, rose again. Ryan remembered Barenwell's saying South Curve was taken in third gear. What was it like to go round this fantastic switchback in the Eiffel mountains at speeds of up to 175 m.p.h., accelerating and braking with such a violence that the world was churned into distorted images?

Two cars, a McLaren and a March, flashed past the pits, their exhaust notes twining together and becoming virtually indistinguishable. The officials, mechanics, team managers, hangers-on, photographers, journalists, TV teams, watched them go by, heads all moving in unison as at a tennis match. Two mechanics held out boards, giving lap times. Following a spin off, a Lotus limped into the pits, nosepiece bent, suspension awry.

The Drew whipped past, engine note harsh and level. Clyne clicked stop-watches and one of the mechanics came up to check the time for the standing lap. Along the pits, a Surtees finally crackled unevenly into life after the mechanics had worked for over half an hour on the fuel lines.

With the suddenness for which the region was notorious, heavy rain fell and the cars, caught on slicks, slowed and came into the pits, except for a Ferrari which spun off and damaged rear suspension on an Armco barrier. Some cars changed to wet-weather tyres and continued, most stayed in the pits with covers over them because with so little practice time left the drivers were reluctant to go out. The clouds pressed down until they wreathed the pine trees, concealed the Schloss Nürburg, and brought to the track an air of Wagnerian doom.

.   .   .   .   .

An hour before the start of the main race the paddock was filled with transporters, cars, people, and noise. Mechanics, ignoring the old maxim to alter or adjust nothing on race day, kept on working and first one car would be started, then another, their vicious, buzz-saw exhaust notes making people nearby cover their ears. Drivers, beseiged by autograph hunters, waited in transporter cabs or at the back of the lock-ups, sitting on piles of wheels. Team managers stood out in the open and stared up at the cloud-filled sky and desperately tried to gauge whether there would be a repetition of yesterday's rain, necessitating wet-weather tyres, whether it would stay fine for slicks, or whether it would drizzle for intermediates: opinions were sought from German officials and police and were found to be completely contradictory.

Ryan, caught up in the fever of the coming race, watched the mechanics as they polished the tiny windscreen and the rims of the wheels of the Drew, carefully making certain not a speck of dirt remained.

Someone spoke in heavily accented English. 'It is a very nice day for car racing.'

He turned. He saw a small, nondescript-looking man, very black-haired and well-moustached, who wore a Tyrolean hat, gaily coloured shirt and leather shorts, and carried a mackintosh. Ryan answered him. 'Especially when so many English cars are competing.'

The man took the package from his mackintosh pocket and handed it over. 'Goodbye.' With unsmiling courtesy, he raised his hat as he spoke. He turned and left and within seconds was swallowed up in the swirling crowd.

Ryan fingered the package with frightened fascination.

.   .   .   .   .

'Something went bang, so I switched the bloody engine off,' said Barenwell to the long-faced, slightly drunk English journalist.

The journalist nodded and walked on, uninterested in failure.

'It's those extra five hundred revs the engines are giving now,' muttered Clyne, for once looking far from cheerful. 'They're costing far too much in reliability.'

As the newly arrived sunlight picked out the oil-stained Drew, Ryan thought how anticlimatic, how useless, a broken-down racing car looked.

'I was closing up with the front runners,' said Barenwell, 'and then the bloody thing went bang and she was like a cow in a gale as the oil reached the tyres.'

'You'd have been right up with them,' said Clyne.

'I'd have been right up with 'em,' he repeated.

Barenwell really needed that reassurance, thought Ryan. The man was a mass of contradictions: ruthless, contemptuous, brave, superstitious, uncertain, surely basically suffering an inferiority complex.

Barenwell looked across the paddock and saw two other drivers with two attractive and strikingly dressed women. He went across and became careless of failure in a sophisticated and amusing manner.

The mechanics pushed the Drew up the ramps into the transporter. Clyne scratched the back of his neck. 'God knows why I stick in this game! Ulcers! —I've got fifty-seven varieties. Look at us now. A broken engine in the car, a broken engine crated up, the spare engine so tired it's yawning, and us with a race next week. Goddamn it, how in the hell am I going to get even one engine back to the factory in time for it to be rebuilt . . .' He suddenly looked at Ryan. 'Know what I'm thinking?'

'I don't need to be a mind reader to do that.'

'Hilary, do me this favour and I'll remember you in all my wills. We'll ship the crated engine by the very next plane. You fly over to meet it and I'll organise a van to take you up to Cosworth. When you get to the factory persuade them with your silver tongue that this is the most important engine on their books and it must be ready by Thursday. They'll say it's impossible. Tell 'em that with Steve driving more brilliantly than ever he's bound to win given a sharp engine and this is their only chance of trouncing the V twelves.'

'I'm on my way.'

'And don't you take any goddamn nonsense from the bloody Customs—make 'em clear it as soon as it arrives even if it's the middle of the goddamn night.'

.   .   .   .   .

It wasn't the middle of the night but seven-thirty in the morning and everyone seemed very tired in the overflow cargo shed at Abston Cross airport.

'I haven't a clue,' said the single-ringed preventive

120

officer from Customs. He meant he didn't give a damn.

Ryan waved the red carbon copy bill of lading. 'It's vitally urgent . . .'

'Everything's urgent, everything's priority. No one seems to care that I . . .' There was a call and he left to go to a tall senior officer.

A fork-lift truck rattled past the crude wooden counter, carrying two small cardboard boxes that surely could have been more easily moved by hand. From outside came the whistling noise of jet engines starting up.

The Customs officer returned, a look of baffled annoyance on his face. 'Will you come this way,' he said.

They walked the length of the shed, a single-span building that had a curiously muffled echo, past piled-up cargo and a caged section for bonded goods. At the far end was the crated Cosworth engine and by it were Foxley and two men, one in uniform. Foxley briefly introduced Detective Sergeant Evans of the local C.I.D. and Brierley, the airport's senior preventive officer from the Custom's waterguard section.

'Will you show us where you've put the package?' asked Foxley.

By the side of the sump there was just room for the package, which he'd coated with oil and grease as camouflage and then taped to the engine. One of the uprights of the open-type crate helped to conceal the place.

Foxley found a piece of cardboard to kneel on. He removed his jacket, rolled up the sleeve of his shirt, and then reached round the crate's upright to bring out the oily package. He handed it to Evans. 'O.K., take it out to check.'

'Yes, sir.' Evans hurried out of the cargo shed, leaving by one of the small doors.

Foxley wiped his hands on one of the hessian-covered packages to the right of the engine and put on his jacket.

'What are you doing?' asked Ryan.

'Making a preliminary analysis of the contents, taking a small sample for further analysis, and checking the wrapping paper for prints.'

'But won't they realise you'll have done all that?'

Foxley smiled. 'No, Mr. Ryan, they won't. I've two experts out in the van who can open anything and reseal it and there aren't half a dozen other men, all forensic scientists, who could tell.' He lit his pipe, although standing immediately under a 'No Smoking' sign.

A party of four men in aircrew uniform crossed the shed, entering by a side door on the south side and leaving by one on the north.

'Who the hell are they?' demanded Foxley, a touch of annoyance in his voice. 'I said we wanted the place kept clear.'

'They're the crew off one of the planes,' replied Brierley. He shrugged his shoulders. 'When the planes are on the south apron they use this shed as a short cut to get to and from their rest and duty rooms. Orders keep going up to stop them, but nothing seems to do that.'

They waited. Ryan thought of Nina and how there'd been a note of strain in her voice when he'd spoken on the phone. What future had they? Would

122

the courts take a lenient view of his past smuggling and let him off very lightly with at the worst a suspended sentence? Would Drew Motors keep him on?

Evans brought them a tray of coffee in chipped mugs: the coffee looked muddy and tasted muddy, but it was hot. After putting his empty mug back on the tray, Foxley checked on the time and then muttered with annoyance and left the shed.

Ryan began to pace the concrete floor and, following Foxley's example, smoked. He tried to start a conversation with Brierley, but the latter, obviously in a bad temper, answered only in monosyllables. Ryan finally gave up and went out of the shed into the early sunshine which as yet had no warmth to it. He began to worry about rushing through the engine: at this rate, the next race would be over and done with before he got it up to Cosworths. He began to walk round the corner of the shed, to find Foxley and ask him to try to hurry things up, but stopped suddenly when he heard Foxley say: 'So it is quinine: I was pretty certain it would be. That means we can let it through.'

Evans spoke. 'The parcel will be ready in about ten minutes.'

'Then we'll go back in and see Ryan.'

Ryan stepped round the corner of the shed. There was a circular road, in the centre of which was a flower-bed with tulips just about to open, and a large plain blue van was parked in the top segment. Foxley and Evans stood by the bonnet, about to leave. Foxley saw Ryan and his mouth tightened slightly.

Ryan went across to where they were. 'What's in that parcel?'

Foxley tapped his pipe on the heel of his shoe and then began to shred tobacco and refill it. He looked up. 'Quinine. Virtually indistinguishable from heroin and what the pushers usually use to cut, or adulterate, it. It adds slightly to the kicks.'

'And you expected it to be quinine?'

'Did I?'

'That's what you said a moment ago.'

'Then that's what I did.'

'Why?'

Foxley struck a match, but could not keep it alight in the breeze which was funnelled at that point by the shape of the buildings. He turned his back to the wind.

'Why did you expect it to be quinine and not heroin?' demanded Ryan again.

There was a rising whoosh of noise as a climbing jet passed overhead.

Foxley got his pipe going. 'All right,' he said to Evans. Evans, after a quick look at Ryan, left.

'They're still trying me out,' said Ryan.

'Maybe.'

'They wanted to check me through for the last time after I tried to quit on them. So that means it must have been quinine I took to New York, not heroin, and you knew that bloody well.'

'So?'

'You lied in order to threaten me into helping you.'

Foxley didn't deny it.

'My run to New York was innocent . . .'

'Innocent?' broke in Foxley, suddenly furious. 'Is that what you're calling it now, in order to salve your miserable little conscience?'

Ryan was shocked by such raw anger in a man usually so calm.

Foxley held the pipe by the bowl. His chin jutted out. 'I've seen more addicts than I like to remember. Youngsters, many of them, twisted into animals: girls of sixteen and seventeen, selling themselves to any pox-ridden man who'll pay enough for the next shot . . . And you were ready to take part in that trade in order to keep up your nice, comfortable standard of living. You were and are as guilty as hell.'

Ryan had lived with his conscience and now could no longer be silenced by it. 'And can you set yourself up on a marble pedestal?' he demanded. 'You're the law, you're justice and truth, yet you deliberately lied to me in order to blackmail me into helping you. So who's the greater bastard?'

Foxley bit down on his pipe.

'You can't arrest me as you threatened. All I've done is smuggle through some quinine. In any case, you wouldn't dare let you part in this become public knowledge. I'm quitting.'

Foxley took the pipe from his mouth. 'You need our help.'

'Why?'

'Because you're still tied in with them. They'll force you to make another run and this time it'll be heroin. We'll pick you up and you'll be jailed for sure because you won't any longer be working for us.'

And if he refused to carry any more packages, the mob would beat up Nina.

Foxley had been watching his face. 'I'll offer you

a deal. We'll agree you've been helping us from the beginning. In return, you'll feed us all the information we need to round up the mob in one clean sweep —which means waiting until you bring through a load of heroin because that's when you'll be watched and we can pick up the watchers.'

Ryan showed his bitter amazement.

'Surprised at such a bargain? Never heard of anything like it in the cloistered, comfortable world in which you've always lived until now?'

'I've always thought . . .' He stopped.

'In the kind of life most of us live, it's eat or be eaten.'

'Shouldn't you say, betray or be betrayed?' corrected Ryan.

15

Nina spoke as she led the way into the bedroom that evening. 'Hilary, did you really accuse that detective of betraying his loyalties?'

'In as many words, yes. It's the truth. Don't you think I ought to have told him?'

'Yes, I do. It's just . . . just you've never before

been the kind of person who can be rude face-to-face.'

He undid his tie, took off his coat and trousers and hung them up in the wardrobe. By the time he was in his pyjamas and in bed she still had only taken off her dress. He watched her. He was totally familiar with her pattern of undressing, the way she bulged as her body was released, yet tonight he knew a pulse-thumping excitement in seeing her growing nakedness, as if this were their first-ever moment of intimacy.

She was about to slip her nightdress over her head when she said: 'Why are you looking at me like that?'

Because she didn't like him to be too openly lustful, he answered as lightly as he could: 'A cat may look at a queen.'

'But you were . . .' She stopped. Quite unconsciously, she held the nightdress so that it provocatively covered half her body.

'Nina,' he said, his voice hoarse.

She dropped the nightdress, crossed to the bed, and climbed in. Then she ceased to be the woman he had known for some years, indulging in sex only in a carefully controlled manner, and became as lasciviously experimental as he, all inhibitions shattered as she moaned her love and her terror of losing him.

Afterwards, as they lay in each other's arms, he remembered Foxley telling him that in the outside world life was red of claw. He could have added that it was also more alive.

127

At ten-thirty on the following Friday, Eccles came into Ryan's office. He refused a chair and sat on the edge of the desk. He had the useful capacity of being able to be completely informal, yet never losing any authority thereby.

Ryan offered a pack of cigarettes and Eccles took one, then flicked open his lighter. 'We're rather pleased with the press coverage you've been getting,' he said.

'That makes nice listening,' replied Ryan, as he sat back in his chair.

Eccles chuckled. 'It's not every firm gets useful publicity from its failures as you did in the *Express*.'

Ryan had angled a two-thousand-word article on the Nürburgring race and the trials and tribulations of the racing mechanics and this had been picked up and used. Readers repeatedly came across the name of Drew and they learned that failure to win the race had been due solely to faulty components not manufactured by Drew Motors.

'How did you enjoy the racing scene?' asked Eccles.

'It's odd. I went expecting almost to be bored because, as you know, I've never followed the sport, yet quite early on I got caught up in all the excitement.'

'It's what happened to me. It's had me wondering whether, despite anything the apologists say, the awareness of disaster, the tingling sensation that this might happen, isn't a large part of that excitement. ... How did you find Steve Barenwell?'

Ryan spoke carefully, not knowing the relationship between the other two. 'A complex character— but can he drive!'

Eccles smiled. 'Very guarded. I'm always sure I should like him a lot more than, in fact, I do.' He slid off the desk. 'Keep up the good work, Hilary.'

After Eccles had gone, Ryan thought how the job fitted him like a glove. The future should be bright. He corrected his thoughts. The future was already bright. No longer was he faced by having to take one of two courses of action, either of which must lead to disaster. Because the police had outsmarted themselves, he was now clear.

The telephone rang at twelve and Smith ordered him to take the package to Abston Cross East railway station on Saturday morning at eleven o'clock and to wait in front of the time-tables of trains up to London. He reported the conversation to Foxley's office. The police wouldn't be covering the handover of the package, he knew, because they wanted no chance of a slip-up at this point. The harmless quinine must be allowed to go through to make it seem that Ryan was the perfect runner, entrapped and browbeaten into submission.

Suppose, he thought with the pleasant fear of a disaster he knew not to have taken place, the gang had decided he was sufficiently trustworthy to have brought heroin in from Germany? Foxley would still have the screws on him. Foxley was sharp, mean, hard, unscrupulous, and unjust in his pursuit of justice. Yet there surely was something to be said for a man who was ready to fight so bitterly against evil?

.   .   .   .   .

Ryan and Nina had just finished supper when the front doorbell rang. Ryan opened the door and found the caller was Comyns.

'I . . .' Comyns cleared his throat. He was standing very erect and there was a strained expression on his austerely lined face.

'Come on in,' said Ryan. Nina entered the hall, said good evening without any welcome in her voice, and went into the kitchen.

It was very obvious that Comyns was suffering a great deal of embarrassment. 'Superintendent Foxley sent me,' he said.

'You know,' said Ryan, 'that man's mind fascinates me. He knows it was your duty to tell him about me and would never begin to countenance your not having done so. But when he's not being as crooked as a Chinese corkscrew, he's highly moral and can't stand betrayed confidences so he's sent you here because it's a job to make your toes curl.'

Comyns stared straight ahead of him, looking at but not seeing the framed etching of early Rushton that was companion to the two in the sitting-room. He spoke jerkily. 'I did my duty.'

'I know.' Ryan suddenly felt sorry for the other, understanding that what he'd done had cost Comyns much painful soul-searching. 'Let me tell you something, Pete. Until recently, I'd cheerfully have kicked you where it hurts. But by telling Foxley what you did, when you did, it turns out you've done me a thumping good turn.'

Comyns looked at Ryan, his expression questioning.

'Come into the sitting-room and we'll have a drink and I'll tell you all.'

By the time Ryan had finished describing what had happened Comyns had completely relaxed, once more at peace with his own conscience. He drank, put down his glass of whisky and soda. 'I'll guarantee you one thing. We'll give you absolute protection, Nina and you, until the whole mob's cleared up and behind bars.'

'That's great. Of course, there won't be any danger now until I bring a load of heroin in and then you should be able to clear everything up before the mob realises what's happening.'

'Nevertheless, we'll take all precautions.' Plainly, Comyns was glad of the chance to do something constructive. 'Hilary, the superintendent wants to know when you're likely to go abroad again?'

Ryan shrugged his shoulders. 'At the moment theres nothing definite.'

'Could there be?'

I suppose so. There's a race in Majorca in three weeks and I could go out with the team.'

'Then if the mob contacts you, will you say you're going there?'

'Sure.'

'Do be careful.'

'I'll be like Agag, only more so.'

.   .   .   .   .

The telephone rang as Ryan was dictating a letter to Madge Jepson. Smith demanded to know when Ryan was next going abroad and where. When Ryan replied Majorca in eighteen days' time. Smith said he'd be ringing back.

Madge Jepson finished taking dictation and went

131

out. With nothing more pressing to do, Ryan reluctantly began to sort through the latest batch of foreign press cutting mentioning Drew cars, sent by representatives in the countries concerned. The directors each month wanted to know how many column inches had appeared in each country as a direct result of articles supplied by his office—a laborious job, even haphazard when he didn't understand a word of the language.

He had lunch in the canteen where the meal was always cheap and sometimes quite tasty. He sat at a table with an accountant and a senior member of the design team who spent much of the meal complaining that his brilliantly conceived project for a mid-engined G.T. car had been abandoned simply because of what the costing department had said, and everybody knew the people who worked there were a load of miserable bastards.

Smith rang again at a quarter to five, just as Ryan put an untitled cutting in the Danish tray because the language looked Scandinavian.

'Stay in Majorca on the Monday.'

Ryan leaned back in his chair and cocked his legs up on the desk. It was amusing to know they thought they'd got him hog-tied whereas in fact he was helping to play them for suckers.

'Go to Cala Rijanus and take the afternoon coach to Saint Fellorca and the exhibition of farmhouse sausage-making. You'll be contacted on the journey and told where to go.'

This was far more complicated than before—confirmation that he'd be carrying heroin this time.

'And listen, mug. Step out of line once and your missus is for it.'

Ryan knew one quick stab of fear as he remembered the blows thudding into his stomach. Then his
confidence returned. 'Don't worry, nothing'll go
wrong.'

16

The newly built Don Ruiz race-track—named after
a Majorcan who towards the end of the sixteenth
century had defeated a raid by Moorish pirates by
means considered very cunning at the time, but now
seldom exactly described—was near Murias, six
miles from Palma. Set out on slightly undulating land
which had until recently grown vines and apricots,
it was 2·3 miles long and shaped like a rectangle
which had been bent out of shape and had buckled
upwards on the north side. Beyond it, forming a
majestic backdrop, were the Sierra de Alfabia mountains, which in sunshine looked peacefully beautiful
but in shadow held a slightly ominous quality.

There had been plans for first-class pits, but somewhere along the line the plans must have been lost
because what were built were primitive boxes, eight
feet by seven and often smelling like lavatories, no
worse but also no better than those found at many
other tracks: the public were allowed to stand on

top of the pits, but had they stopped to consider the method of construction they might have chosen not to do so. Only two of the projected stands had as yet been completed and these two lacked roofs, but in such a climate that was of small consequence except to those who disliked the sun.

Competing cars were flown to the island by specially chartered aircraft and then brought from Palma airfield to Murias by whatever means of transport were available: one harassed team manager, finding damaged suspension, swore his two cars had been brought on a donkey cart fitted with square wheels. The paddock was open to the public, so the cars and all their accompanying equipment were fenced off with metal and rope barriers, neither of which were entirely successful in keeping at bay the hordes of Majorcan youths who were speed crazy.

For the Drew team, practice was all trouble. First, there was heavy tyre vibration, especially on the fast bends where the inside wheel was lightly loaded, presumed to be caused by the enormous size and the profile of the new slicks. Stays cracked, were repaired and strengthened, cracked again: dampers were fitted. Then in the second practice session Barenwell came round Mahon Bend and ran over a dog as it tried to cross the track: a tyre punctured, the car spun off and sliced along some Armco barrier to wreck the right front suspension. The already weary mechanics had to work throughout the night to repair the suspension and fit the race engine.

The start of the race was a shambles. The cars, in three, two, three formation, were called up from the dummy grid at the one minute signal and slotted into their grid positions. Señor Jorge Vartalitis, a visiting dignitary from Buenos Aires, stepped up on to the rostrum and held the Spanish flag ready as the thirty-, twenty-, and ten-second signals were given by klaxon and board: at five seconds, with all the drivers blipping at over 7000 revs as the tension gripped them, first gears engaged and clutches just biting, Señor Vartalitis raised the flag.

Revs rose higher, marked for drivers only by tachometers and vibration because individual exhaust and engine notes were lost in the maelstrom of noise. Señor Vartalitis seemed suddenly to lower the flag slightly, then he held it steady. Some cars shot forward, their tyres just spinning but not enough to burn off much rubber, others stayed put. There were three collisions. Then the flag swept right down and all but two of the cars snaked off, leaving behind them a blast of hot air, rubber, smoke, and noise. Señor Vartalitis excitedly explained that he'd almost tripped off the rostrum at the vital moment and that that was why the flag had jerked: he expressed surprise that the drivers of the cars couldn't realise what had happened. The drivers of the two wrecked cars, both from Australia, expressed their opinions of Señor Vartalitis in terms which would have ensured trouble had any of the nearby police or officials understood their vivid phrases.

Barenwell battled for the lead for six laps, at his best in the middle of a dog-fight and being spurred on by his highly competitive nature, driving that little closer to the limit than he would ever do when out on his own. Twice he held the lead from a B.R.M. and a Lotus, outcornering both on the tricky left-handed Pollença Curve where braking

135

dropped their speeds from 170 to 70 m.p.h. in under two hundred yards and they'd changed from fifth through fourth to third. Each time on the following mile-long straight the V12 B.R.M. went by and the Lotus came alongside to challenge for the line for the following left-hander. On the seventh lap the Drew's engine went badly off song, dropped a thousand revs., and Barenwell's race was over.

Ryan watched the Drew come up the pit lane, engine sounding really rough. As it stopped, the three mechanics and Clyne surrounded it and Barenwell blipped the engine once and then cut it. Clyne straightened up, the mechanics stepped back, Barenwell climbed out of the cockpit, removed goggles, helmet, flameproof mask, and ear plugs, and without a backward look at the car jumped down into the pit and went through there to the paddock and the van which Clyne had hired. Barenwell was not a man who could treat either triumph or disaster as an imposter. One of the mechanics climbed into the cockpit of the Drew and the other two pushed the car along the pit lane, down the ramp, and round through the quickly opened gateway to the paddock.

Ryan looked up at the clock in the centre of the SEAT Tower, which housed timekeepers, race commentators, journalist, and V.I.P. guests. Nearly three o'clock. This time tomorrow he would be on the bus. The woman at the tourist centre had told him that although this wasn't really the sausage-making season, the whole process was carried out exactly as it would be closer to Christmas and was, she said, very illuminatory.

.   .   .   .   .

The Hotel Coral Playa in Puerto Segusa consisted of an old and elegant two-storey Spanish-style building to which had been added a twelve-storey concrete-and-glass block—somehow the two parts merged into one and the one retained a mellow charm. Ryan walked down the main staircase and into the lobby, passing under the curved archway, supported by two simply carved pillars, across which grew a very prolific plant whose main stem sent out myriads of roots which unavailingly clawed at the stonework. The desk clerk, foot in plaster from a recent fall, smiled a welcome: incredibly, all the staff were pleasant and nothing was too much trouble for them.

He passed the dining-room, where most of the guests were still eating, and went outside: maids were sweeping up the floor of the verandah-like front —never before had he stayed in such a clean hotel. He crossed the road and unlocked the driving door of the 1500 SEAT he'd hired, sat down behind the wheel and stared out at the hotel's private beach square, furnished with deck-chairs and overhead rush sun mats, the two-hundred-yard concrete pier, the blue sea and sky, and the red sails of the dinghies lazily moving from the harbour. It was more like a travel poster than most travel posters.

The SEAT's engine fired at the fourth attempt, not bad going for a car which obviously was close to pensioning-off time. He engaged reverse, backed out, and carried on along the sea road past other hotels and several shops which catered almost exclusively for tourists and whose prices were high.

The road from Puerto Segusa to Cala Rijanus ran over hills, bare and prehistoric-looking, that offered soaring views down sheer cliffs to the azure blue sea, and then descended into a pine-covered valley which led out on to the sea-front, which, unlike the eastern approach, was unspoilt by a rash of hotels, chalets, and apartment blocks. The narrow, sandy beach which lay partially beneath pine trees and the sea incredibly was even bluer than at Puerto Segusa.

The coach station, which turned out to be no more than a large cobbled square by the small harbour in which were tied up a number of fishing boats, was well filled with vehicles and even while he was searching for the Saint Fellorca coach two more arrived and disembarked German and Italian tourists.

The coach left Cal Rijanus by the east road, passing through the depressing area of modern tourist development, and then crossed the flat, browned land of small fields which contained corn or stubble, often under the ubiquitous almond trees, sheep and goats, some lucern, apricot orchards, and sprawling clumps of cactus. In Saint Fellorca they parked by the side of a monastery with tall, sheer walls unbroken by windows and a bell tower which leaned several degrees out of the perpendicular.

' 'Alf an hour we stay,' said the courier, a bumptious, cocky man, whose English was fractured and whose French was most peculiar. 'Shoes are very O.K. You shop there.' He pointed across the road.

Ryan was last but one off the bus and he walked across the sun-drenched, airless street towards what looked like a café, though in an old town like this where shops were often identifiable only by the strings of beads at open doorways to keep off flies, it was difficult for a visitor to be certain. As he reached

138

the pavement, a small, dark-skinned man, who'd not been on the bus, joined him. 'Hullo, Mr. Ryan.' His voice was soft and he tended to hiss as if he had ill-fitting teeth.

Ryan knew he must have been identified from the photograph and this small fact strangely reinforced very forcibly something he'd really only come to appreciate recently—the organisation was large by any standards and therefore had to maintain a degree of efficiency no commercial business would disdain.

'You are having a pleasant stay in Mallorca, Mr. Ryan?' The man smiled quickly, showing gold-capped front teeth. 'Mr. Ryan, when you get back to Cala Rijanus, you will drive to Santa Maria and take the west road towards Orient. Three kilometres after Algendar you will see the ruins of a house on the left. Continue to the next bend and wait. Your contact will drive up and say "Good afternoon" and you will reply "Good morning" and he will give you the package.' The man smiled again, turned, and walked briskly along the pavement for twenty-five yards to a side road.

Ryan continued on to the café, only to discover it wasn't one, and the heat seemed to draw the last beads of moisture out of him. He wondered if any drinks would be served at the demonstration of butifarra- and sobresada-making—the latter, he'd been told, a raw, red mixture guaranteed to put any Englishman off sausages for life.

17

Even in the shade of the pine trees the heat was heavy and sweat rolled down Ryan's face and the small of his back as he stared down at the man on the ground whom he now identified as one of the aircrew who'd taken a short cut through the cargo shed at Abston Cross airport when he'd been showing Foxley where the package had been hidden in the crated Cosworth engine.

There was the small tinkle of a bell and Ryan whipped round and stared past a thicket of browned gorse which had grown where several pine trees had fallen, but he saw nothing. He turned back and willed the man to move, even as he acknowledged the futility of this. The man was dead.

With the far-seeing clarity that came from stark tension, he appreciated most of the implications of what had happened. If he reported the death to the Spanish authorities he must be held, and in the context of admitted drug-smuggling what chance was there of a successful plea of self-defence: not to mention God knows how many years of imprisonment for attempted smuggling? Foxley wouldn't be able to do much, even if he wanted to: perhaps he'd like to see Ryan in real trouble. If he hid the body and left, he was safe only until the mob were identified and arrested and they learned they'd been double-crossed by him and that he'd been working for the police. At that point, they'd know their missing first runner must somehow have uncovered Ryan's double-cross and have been killed by him. Ryan would be on a murder charge just as quickly as they could get him there.

Once again, he was in the nightmare position of having to take one of two courses of action, either of which must lead to disaster. He looked at the body and hated the dead man with a violence that prevented almost any feeling of revulsion. Surely there had to be something he could do? He lit a cigarette and noticed his hands were hardly shaking. Nine months ago, no one could have persuaded him that he could kill a man. . . .

As the sun swung overhead, sharp sunlight slipped between two pine trees to cover the dead man's back and Ryan saw the coat was translucent. He dragged the smoke down into his lungs and tried to force his battered mind into action. A plane droned across the sky, leaving behind vapour trails as it suddenly and starkly reintroduced the twentieth century.

There were more tinkling bells from unseen sheep or goats and Ryan became terrified a shepherd would stumble on the scene, but his isolation remained. The bloody fool of a man, he thought: why had he panicked and tried to kill, which had led to his own death?

He had only one possible course of action left. Once again, to avert the nearer disaster even if that inevitably meant he must become caught up by the other.

No one other than the mob knew about this meeting. But the dead man had come in a car. When it was known he was missing, the police would make enquiries and the abandoned car would start a search in the immediate area. So either the car or the body had to be moved.

He bent down and put his hands under the shoulder blades of the dead man and tried to lift: he might have been struggling to raise something that was lead-filled. He dropped in to the ground. The man's head jerked round to show his right profile and Ryan thought how disgusting the heavily plastered-down, lank black hair looked.

He left the body and began to explore the area and twenty yards back found what looked like the remains of a brick-built well, twelve feet across, now with collapsed sides, and a half-tumbledown building to the right.

Returning to the body, he took a firm grip on it and began to pull. This time, perhaps because he now had a definite objective, he managed more easily and made progress up the slight slope, stopping twice to rest and wipe away copious sweat. Reaching the lip of the well, he was about to push the body over when he remembered the knife which must be covered with his fingerprints.

He turned the body on to its back. The man's eyes and mouth were open and he seemed to have a fixed smile, showing very white teeth. Ryan gripped the knife and began to pull. There was a trickle of mucky blood, a squishing noise, and he had the sensation of actually being able to feel the metal slide against the torn flesh. Suddenly shocked, he nearly vomited.

When the knife was free, he kicked the man over the side of the well. The body fell on to the bricks with a soft, thumping sound. Ryan cleaned the knife in the ground and wiped the handle again and again with his handkerchief. He carefully put the knife down, then went to the tumbledown building and threw loose bricks into the well until, hands raw in places and muscles aching, the body was finally out of sight.

He carried the knife back to his SEAT and only then was frightened by the possibility that the keys of the second SEAT were in one of the pockets of the dead man. He ran the few feet to the second car and knew breath-easing relief when he saw the keys in the dashboard. He picked up the package on the passenger seat and put it in his pocket.

He had no gloves. He used a handkerchief to open the door and then, when seated, that handkerchief and a second one to start the engine, release the handbrake, steer, and change gear.

The road twisted up one side of a pine-covered hill and down the other. There were no houses, no people, nothing but the trees which covered the road with dappled shadows. Beyond the hill, as the road turned a hair-pin, he saw ahead and to the left a few fields which, stretching part way up a slope and enclosed by dry-stone walls, were under cultivation. He stopped the car because somewhere around there were likely to be farm workers, with the pin-point accurate memories of simple people: in any case, the odometer recorded nearly two kilometres and, in woods as thick as these, two kilometres ought to be more than enough to prevent any search being successful.

He left the keys in the dashboard, wiped down steering-wheel, handbrake, and gear shift, even though there could be no possibility of his having implanted a fingerprint, and climbed out of the car.

143

The scent of thyme and lavender was strong. He walked back along the road, confident he would hear the approach of any vehicle in plenty of time to take cover.

Back at his own SEAT the solitude was unbroken when he arrived, but even as he sat down behind the wheel he heard the buzzing approach of another car. A small Simca came round the bend behind him, continued past and out of sight, driving in the middle of the road. Something about the look of the driver, perhaps his lobster-red face, suggested he was English, unlikely to be interested in the parked car, probably forgetting all about it soon after passing.

Ryan drove off. He reached the SEAT of the dead man, tried not to look at it too closely and continued to the next bend at which was a tall carob tree. His last glimpse of the car in the rear-view mirror showed everything to be quiet.

The road began a long climb up from the foothills into the mountains and he reached a rocky plateau, five hundred yards long, a precipitous fall to the left, littered with a multitude of boulders which had crashed down from the cliff face behind it. He left the car and walked amongst the boulders and thirty yards in, behind a boulder five feet high and shaped like a pumpkin, he found a cleft in the rock that was almost four inches wide and of unknown but obviously considerable depth. He dropped the knife down this.

.   .   .   .   .

There was a knock on Ryan's hotel-room door and the waiter brought in a champagne cocktail. He

144

asked Ryan to sign the chit for the drink and thanked him with a smile in which there was no suggestion of tiredness even though he had been on duty for sixteen hours.

Ryan carried the drink over to the opened window where a breeze was coming in from the sea, dispelling some of the heat, and sat down on a rickety wooden chair. The moon was nearly full and it sent shafts of rippling light across the water: to the left, the lighthouse occulted every six seconds; to the right, the lights of the harbour were doubled by reflection. What in the hell was he going to do? he thought, his dilemma seemingly made more acute by the quiet beauty of the scene.

He'd made an agreement with the police and was honour bound by it. By honouring it and handing over the heroin on arrival in England, he must inevitably be inculpated in the murder of the dead man. There was no way out.

He finished his drink and quite abruptly realised that he was being a naive fool. He no longer belonged to a world where a man's word was his bond. If he could successfully double-cross the police he would buy himself time: time meant hope.

Twenty minutes later, he picked up the telephone and asked the man at the desk to put through a call to Rushton three eight three eight two. There was a long wait, a series of clicks, scraps of Spanish, a short and angry-sounding speech in what was probably Majorcan, an English voice which asked if he were trying to call Rushton and then vanished for good when he answered yes, more Spanish, and a comment from the desk clerk that sometimes events took a little time. He sweated as he waited and worked out all that could go wrong with his plan.

'Hullo . . . hullo.' Nina's voice was filled with worry.

'Hullo, darling.'

'What's wrong?'

'Nothing very much. But I've changed my mind and would like you to meet me at the airport tomorrow.'

'Of course, but you said . . .'

'Sit down close to the news-stand in the centre of the general lounge. Don't move. Don't speak to me and grab what I give you. Hide it and leave immediately. Give the package to your aunt in Ashton and tell her to guard it as carefully as she's always guarded her virtue.'

'But what . . . ?'

'It's all sorting itself out, darling. So there's no need to worry.' He rang off and mopped his face and neck with a handkerchief.

18

The plane touched down on time and came to a stop by the disembarkation pier. Ryan followed a very plump woman down the steps from the plane and up the steps to the covered passage and he noticed she had four pimples in the back of her neck that formed a perfect square.

The Immigration officer skimmed through his passport and handed it back. He walked into the Customs hall, found his suitcase on the luggage belt, and crossed to the line of desks for those with something to declare. Detective Sergeant Evans was standing by the nearest desk.

'What have you to declare?' asked the Customs officer.

'I bought a few things in Palma,' answered Ryan. 'They're all in my suitcase.' He wondered if his appearance was betraying the tight nervousness that filled him and if Evans would have the imagination to read any special significance in it.

'Open up, then, please.'

On top of his clothes was a gaily wrapped package and inside this was a brown paper package he'd sealed with sealing-wax and which contained quinine powder he'd bought that morning in Palma. In his right trouser pocket, feeling the size of a gatepost, was the sealed package which had come from the dead man's car.

'What's in this?' asked the Customs officer, indicating the package. He spoke with obvious irritation, annoyed at having to take part in what he considered to be stupid play-acting.

'Some Majorcan pearls I bought in Manacor.'

'We'll have to examine them to assess their value for duty. Have you the receipt?' Evans picked up the package, took a piece of paper from Ryan, crossed to a doorway to his right and went through.

The Customs officer left to question an elderly,

147

bearded man who was travelling with a seemingly endless array of cases.

Evans returned and handed Ryan the package which Ryan knew must now contain the quinine which the police had substituted for what they were so certain was heroin; they'd made the substitution before their analyses were made.

'That'll be four pounds fifty,' Evans said. 'And add twenty-five quid extra for me,' he continued in a stage whisper, exposing himself as a man with a sense of humour.

Ryan counted out five pounds. Evans gave him a fifty-pence piece in change and a receipt. Foxley had carefully promised the money would be returned later.

Ryan went into the general hall which was thronged with people. He knew that amongst the genuine holidaymakers were detectives, watching and waiting for any contact, and in addition it was a fifty-fifty chance the mob would also be there because he was carrying uncut heroin worth about eighty-five thousand pounds when it reached the States.

Nina was on one of the low bench-type settees, to the left of the news-stand. There was a free seat by her side and he sat down almost before she'd seen him. He draped his mackintosh between them and under its cover pulled from his pocket the package of heroin. She took it from him.

She bundled the package into her plastic shopping bag, stood up and smoothed down her skirt in a typically femine gesture, and walked away. He was amazed that anyone as essentially nervous as she could act so naturally. Tensed, he watched her until she walked through the main exit doors.

He smoked and wondered how long it would be before the police reacted. Then he dropped the cigarette butt into a tall ashtray and left.

Immediately outside the main exit doors was a covered way and to the left of this was the boarding point for the coaches which maintained a shuttle service between the airport and central Abston Cross and to the right was a taxi-rank. He walked towards the leading taxi and a blue Viva cut in ahead of them. The driver—whom he didn't know—shouted through the opened passenger window: 'Hullo there, Hilary. Have you been abroad? Going into town? Climb in and I'll give you a lift.'

He sat down in the front passenger seat. They made a U-turn, drove down the slight ramp and round to the main London/Abston Cross road. 'Superintendent Foxley wants a word with you,' said the driver, as he waited at the traffic lights.

'Is something up, then?' asked Ryan. 'He told me there'd be no direct contact before I returned to my house.'

'Search me. I'm just the erk who does as he's told.'

Ryan noticed the driver kept glancing in the rearview mirror and after a time he became certain he could make out a following Triumph 2000, driven by Foxley. That he was correct was confirmed when, on entering the town, they drove through a maze of back streets and the Triumph stayed with them.

County police H.Q. was to the east of the town, on the outskirts and just beyond one of the fashionable suburbs. The main building was Regency in style, with two wings, and built in pleasant pink-tinted bricks: also on the fifty-acre site were hostel, driving school, playing fields, and a number of police houses.

Foxley's office was on the third floor of the main building, a large room he obviously shared with another man, painted in institutional shades of brown. Foxley was standing by one of the windows and Evans was sitting on a chair. The driver of the Vauxhall, who'd stayed with Ryan during the ten-minute wait below, put Ryan's suitcase in the centre of the room and left.

'What's caused the sudden change in plans?' asked Ryan, trying a little too hard to be vaguely surprised.

Foxley, his square face almost expressionless, studied him for several seconds, then pointed with the stem of the pipe he held in his right hand. 'Have a seat.'

Ryan sat down.

Foxley brought his battered tobacco pouch out of his pocket and carefully shredded tobacco, then filled the pipe. He lit up. 'Now just tell me very simply,' he said, in his most avuncular manner, 'what incredible idea you've schemed up? Then we'll have to try and sort things out.'

Foxley, thought Ryan, really should have been a salesman: he could even have sold the Llanarch Hamal to the Americans.

'You know, Mr. Ryan, you're lucky. If I weren't something of a patient man, I could get pretty annoyed.'

'I'm sorry,' replied Ryan, 'but I don't know what you mean.'

Foxley sighed. 'You've done a switch on the heroin.'

150

'Done what?'

Foxley's voice abruptly hardened, as it sometimes did when momentarily he couldn't quite hide his anger. 'The package we took from you at the airport contained quinine and not heroin.'

'But you said that this trip I was bound to be carrying heroin.'

'Right.'

'But now you're saying it isn't right?'

Foxley's voice resumed its former pleasant tone. 'Do you remember the bargain we struck? Struck because I was prepared, despite what had happened, to treat you as a man of honour?

'Of course.'

'Then don't let me down.'

'But I haven't.'

'I know you've switched quinine for the heroin you were given to bring into this country.'

'Look, I was given a package, I wrapped it up in some bright paper and I brought it back and handed it over.'

'Tell me why you've betrayed my trust in you? Is it because you're afraid we shan't arrest everyone and therefore won't be able to protect you and your wife?'

'I tell you, I haven't switched anything.'

'Surely you can't have been such a fool as to decide to try to muscle into the profits of dope smuggling?' Foxley sounded shocked that it was even remotely possible anyone could be that stupid and he looked across at Evans as if seeking confirmation of his own surprise.

'How many more times do I have to tell you I've done nothing?'

Foxley smoked a while. He took the pipe out of his mouth. 'I'll never understand people,' he said heavily. 'And to think I was gullible enough to trust you . . .' He spoke to Evans. 'You'd better search his suitcase.'

Evans searched the suitcase with meticulous care, checking measurements for a secret compartment, tapping all the lining, unrolling every item of clothing and examining all the seams, opening the leather purse that Ryan had bought for Nina and poking around in the rubber flippers that were for Jack. 'Nothing,' he reported. He repacked the suitcase.

Foxley walked from the window to the seat behind his desk. He tapped the bowl of the pipe, which had gone out, up and down on the palm of his hand. 'Unless you see reason, you'll have to be personally searched. I think you ought to know that for a man of your background it's likely to be rather a humiliating experience.'

'I've lied about nothing.'

They searched him.

Foxley spoke to Evans. 'Who was in the main hall?'

'Phil, sir.'

'Go and get him.'

Phil was in his middle or late twenties, quick, sharp-eyed, and very confident in manner. He read out of his notebok a description of all Ryan's movements up to the time he climbed into the Viva.

Foxley drummed on the desk with his fingers. 'Why did you go and sit down in the lounge?' he asked Ryan.

Ryan shrugged his shoulders. 'Why not?'

Foxley spoke to Phil again. 'Are you positive he didn't talk to anyone?'

'Absolutely, sir.'

'Who else was on the seat with him?'

Phil did not answer immediately and it was clear he had to think back, not having made a note of this point. 'There was one woman.'

'When did she leave?'

'Very soon after Ryan sat down.'

'Describe her.'

Phil detailed a woman in her middle thirties, of average height, attractive, long face, brown hair, wearing a print dress.

Ryan wondered why the description was so very inaccurate and then realised he was lucky because Phil was the kind of cockily confident man who'd never willingly admit he'd fallen down on his job and didn't know something he should.

'Why won't you believe the truth—that they were making one more dummy run?' demanded Ryan.

Foxley stared at him.

'May I go now?'

'Yes.'

'Can someone drive me to the station?'

Foxley jerked his head at Phil. 'Take him.' He could not hide his final uncertainty.

.   .   .   .   .

Ryan crossed to the cocktail cabinet and poured himself out a second strong gin and tonic. He found he could not keep silent. 'And d'you know the thing that really frightens me, Nina?'

She shook her head.

153

'I'm horrified by what I did and yet . . .'

She ran her tongue along her lips. 'Yet what?'

'Yet I feel even a little elated at having done something so terrible and exceptional, as if I were someone dreamed up by Dostoïevski.'

She shivered and he went over and put his hand on her shoulder.

.   .   .   .   .

Ryan was at work when Smith rang.

'So how did the trip go?'

'As smooth as the others.'

'You've got the goods?'

'Yes.'

There was a pause, then: 'No sort of trouble?'

'None at all. Things couldn't have been smoother.'

Another pause. 'Tomorrow afternoon at three o'clock in Trafalgar Square. Wait by the fountain, on the side of the National Gallery. When you're asked if you've been abroad, say you've just spent a week in Athens.'

19

Ryan left Charing Cross Station and, together with a dozen other people, waited on the pavement until the policeman on point duty stopped traffic coming along the Strand to let three taxis drive out of the station forecourt. He walked along to the lights, which were in his favour, and crossed to the central island.

The day was only partially sunny because of cumulus cloud, but it was warm and there were a large number of tourists in colourful clothes feeding the pigeons and providing peanut vendors and photographers with brisk trade.

He walked round the fountain, stood just clear of the odd damping of spray the wind sent over, and remembered exactly what he'd told Nina the night before. It was ironic that his sense of guilt stemmed mainly from not being more ashamed of his actions, not from the actions themselves. His mind and sense of morality had become warped out of shape. A year ago, he could be absolutely certain of his honesty: now, all that guided him was self-preservation.

How near was he to preserving himself? He'd won some time, but it couldn't be much. The mob, if he could convince them he knew nothing about the missing man in Majorca, would demand he continued to work for them as a runner. The police would never again let him trick them. The inevitability of disaster remained, only its timing had been altered.

A man, very bald for his age, paunch straining

155

his trousers, no coat and in shirtsleeves, rolled up, skin glistening with sweat. 'Been abroad at all, mate?'

'I'm just back from Athens where I spent a week.'

'Let's 'ave it, then.'

Ryan put his hand in his coat pocket.

'Stop looking round. D'you want every bleeding flatfoot in the manor to come running?'

He realised he'd automatically searched for the nearest policeman to see if they were being watched. He passed over the package.

'And this is your bundle.'

He was handed a large brown envelope, folded in half. The balding man left, crossing to the pavement to the west side of the square. Ryan walked aimlessly away from the fountain and up the double flight of stairs to the road. He crossed to the National Gallery, went in, and turned right into Gallery 13.

He sat down on one of the black upholstered seats, unfolded the envelope, and slit the flap with his thumb. Inside was a bundle of five-pound notes. A very rough count suggested there were about a thousand pounds.

He stared at Degas' *The Toilet*. From the moment he'd killed the man on the road to Orient, he'd been so completely wrapped up in the problem of survival that he'd never given a thought to the money the mob would pay him. Even though Foxley wouldn't believe him one iota more, he must hand the money over to sustain his part as a man still working with the police. In any case, the alternative was to destroy it because it was tainted money and he now knew and acknowledged this.

.   .   .   .   .

They jumped him that night as he was walking back home from having posted a letter after dinner and it was obvious they'd been watching the house. A car drew alongside the pavement just behind him and even as he turned a man got out and he felt the point of a knife biting through his clothes to prick his flesh: in a flash, he vividly remembered how the knife had slid into the man's body to kill him. There was a muttered order to get into the car and he did so. They drove off. It had all happened so quickly and slickly that the only other pedestrian, going in the same direction on the other side of the road, had obviously noticed nothing suspicious.

They pulled a hood over his head and pinned him in the back seat, between two of them. The car stopped at the T-junction at the end of the road and turned right. He tried to follow their route from there, but before long gave up when he realised he'd lost any sense of orderly direction.

After a quarter of an hour's run they came to a stop and the engine was switched off. His hood was roughly removed. There were four men in the car, one on either side of him and two in the front. Outside, a distant street light showed him rough grass and horsechestnut trees and he guessed they were parked on one of the commons, probably Barming Common. The man on his left held the knife close to his side, but not actually touching it.

The man in the front passenger seat turned round, his face looking grotesquely evil under the nylon mask. 'What happened?' he demanded roughly.

Ryan found himself scared, yet unlike the last time they'd grabbed him he was now able to think coherently and to evaluate what he was going to say.

'How d'you mean? Happened where?'

'In Majorca, you stupid bastard.' The accent of the speaker was recognisably Birmingham.

'I did exactly as you told me.'

'So now tell us about it.'

He briefly described the coach journey to the sausage-making farm, the contact, and the meeting with the other runner. He said that as soon as the package was handed to him, he'd returned to his car and driven off.

'What was this other bloke doing when you left?'

Ryan decided to risk the old dodge of giving credence to a lie by detailing something so unexpected the listener was surprised into believing it. 'Picking flowers.'

'What?'

'Picking some little pink flowers like Ragged Robin that were growing close to the road.'

'Jesus!' said the speaker. He was silent for several seconds. 'Where d'you go?'

'I returned straight to my hotel—in Puerto Segura.'

'Did he say anything to you before you drove on?'

Ryan appeared to think back. 'He talked a bit about the pine woods being beautiful and how the flowers reminded him of home. He didn't say where home was.'

'He didn't talk about nothing else?'

'No.'

'And he gave you the package?'

'Well, of course he did—how else could I have passed it on to the man in London? Has something happened?'

The driver spoke for the first time, his voice sharp.

158

'Hal, there's a cruising flatcar coming up.'

The tension was immediate. The knife was pressed against Ryan's side and he felt the prick of its point against the soft flesh between hip and lowest rib. With the others, he watched the white patrol car cruise along the road at right angles to the one they were on.

When the patrol car was out of sight, the point of the knife was withdrawn. The man in the front passenger seat turned and looked at Ryan. 'When you left, he was just picking flowers?'

'That's right.' They knew the man was missing, he thought, but until they learned he'd been working with the police they could have no real reason for suspecting he had a motive for murder.

'Get out. Walk straight off across the grass and don't look back.'

He climbed over the legs of the man on his right, who made no effort to move them, opened the door and stepped out into the warm night air. He walked across the grass and beneath a tree whose branches spread out in a large canopy and heard the car drive off.

He was very soon able to confirm it was Barming Common. After a reasonably short wait, a number sixteen A bus took him within four minutes of Thorndale House.

Nina was frantic with worry. 'What happened? Where have you been, Hilary? You said you were only going out to post a letter.'

He shut the front door before answering her. 'They picked me up again.' He crossed to where she stood and put his arms round her. 'It's all right, my darling, all they did was ask questions. I told you they'd probably do that.'

'Did they believe what you told them?'

'D'you think I'd be here if they hadn't?'

She shivered. 'I was so worried . . . I nearly phoned the police . . .'

Her dilemma had been acute. Had he been caught up in some 'ordinary' accident when to call the police for help was the obvious thing to do, or had the mob picked him up so that the police were the last people to be told? He kissed her. He tried to give her no inkling of the fact that the problems which still faced them were as apparently insoluble as ever.

20

Ryan drove from the Drew factory to the nearby town—a small, pleasant place, still fairly rural in character, noted for the very wide, tree-lined main street—and went into the National Westminster Bank to cash a cheque for ten pounds. As the cashier briskly counted out ten one-pound notes, he wondered about the thousand pounds he didn't know what to do with.

Near the bank was a small jeweller's where the previous week he'd seen a tiny elephant in silver, made to fit on to a charm ring. He went in and bought it for Nina. Afterwards, he walked along the pavement, set between shops and a twenty-foot-wide grass verge in which grew flowering trees, to a small Italian restaurant where the food was good yet very reasonably priced.

As he ate the antipasti, he thought about time: the measure he'd brought himself must be about running out. Soon, the mob would call on him to act as runner again.

The waiter, swarthy and with long curly black hair, cleared away the empty plate. Ryan poured himself out a second glassful of wine from the green carafe and lit a cigarette. Yet again, for the umpteenth time, how to avoid the unavoidable?

His main dish arrived: kidneys cooked in garlic, fried potatoes, and Brussels sprouts. It was a highly anti-social dish because of the amount of garlic the cook used, but it was delicious. What did food in prison taste like? How would Nina manage? . . . So similar to the questions he'd asked himself months ago, when Chapel at Llanarchs had finally gained his revenge.

He was chewing the last piece of kidney when the idea hit him, thrown up nearly complete, proving his subconscious had been working on the problem all the time.

It was a good idea which slotted in neatly to all the facts and promised him a way out of the inescapable. Yet, now he came to examine it in greater detail, he recognised there was one reason why it couldn't succeed. Events might have changed him from a man practising the conventional honesty of those who could afford such luxury to one concerned only in survival and to whom truth, justice, and

161

honour, were all variables, but what events had not done was to teach him the art of being a criminal.

He finished the wine. The waiter removed the plate, the side-plate, and the remains of the roll, and took his order of a lemon sorbet. He stared at a crude mural of an Elysian Mediterranean scene on the far wall and cursed because he had the solution but not the means of expediting it.

The sorbet was delicious. The waiter asked if he'd like a liqueur with coffee and he chose a strega. He was sipping the strega when he suddenly—and silently—shouted Eureka! The solution had been staring him in the face, only it had taken him all this while to realise it . . . The thousand pounds he couldn't decide what to do with.

He knew one potentially vital piece of information that he himself couldn't follow up but which might identify the leader of the mob—information which, ironically, couldn't have come to him had he not killed the man in Majorca and so set the mob a problem they couldn't solve. But if he couldn't follow it up, he could bribe someone else who could. The mob had made him an expert in knowing how a man's honesty could be skilfully seduced.

It would make for a nice circle: bribery, smuggling, murder, smuggling, and return to bribery.

Ryan ran his finger down the long list of Joneses in the telephone directory and eventually found the address: Jones Detective Agency, 14 Madders Road,

Abston Cross. He shut the directory, left the telephone kiosk, and returned to his car.

Madders Road was on the outskirts of the centre of Abston Cross and the businesses there were those which couldn't afford a high rent but which had to be as close as possible to other and more prosperous ones. Number fourteen was a tall, thin building, one of an ugly block built in yellow bricks, and the detective agency was on the second floor. There were two rooms, the first used by a cross-eyed secretary in mournful middle age and the other by Jones. Each room was furnished as cheaply as was possible.

The secretary showed Ryan into the second room and Jones shook hands limply.

Ryan sat down on the plain wooden chair and stared at Jones, whose ears and face were still unusually red and whose expression remained one of resigned pessimism. 'Do you remember me?'

Jones fiddled with his upper lip as he struggled to identify his caller without making this too obvious.

'We last met at Llanarch Motors.'

'Yes, of course, Mr. Ryan.' Jones became nervous: was Ryan a potential client or had he come to cause trouble?

'I've some work I'd like you to do for me.'

Jones' manner crystallised. 'Only too happy, Mr. Ryan.' He energetically nodded his over-large head.

'It's confidential work.'

'All my work is confidential, in a manner of speaking.'

'I'm talking about every manner of speaking.'

Jones cleared his throat noisily.

163

'I'm in trouble with several people,' said Ryan, 'including the police.'

Jones ran his fingers through his lank brown hair, tinged with orange lights from recent faulty dyeing. He cleared his throat again. 'I am not prepared to do anything illegal.' He waited, but when Ryan was silent, he added: 'As a private detective of nearly thirty years' standing, I observe the most rigorous rules of . . .'

Ryan interrupted the other's pompous words. 'I'm not asking you to break the law.'

'Oh! But you said . . .'

'I said I was in trouble with the police. That's all.' Ryan took his bulging wallet from his pocket. 'What are your charges?'

Jones moistened his lips, looked quickly at Ryan, then away. 'Twenty pounds a day,' he said, striving not to sound too hopeful.

'Three days' work is sixty pounds.' Ryan opened the wallet and counted out twelve five-pound notes. He put them on the desk. 'I want some information.'

'What kind?'

'I need to identify a criminal.'

'Surely the police are the people . . .'

'I told you, I'm in trouble with them.' Ryan riffled the edge of the notes with his thumb.

Jones fiddled with the lobe of his right ear. 'Exactly what is it you want to know?'

'The identity of a man who's in the dope racket who's called Hal by his companions and who speaks with a Brummagem accent.'

'Records in the county force might be able to identify the man from that, Mr. Ryan, or the national ones in London, but as I said earlier on you need

164

to go to the police. I can't ask Records . . .'

'I'm sure you know someone in the police who could make an enquiry for you?'

'Of course I know one or two blokes, but they can't do that sort of thing. You must understand, it's highly confidential information . . .'

Ryan produced his wallet again. He counted out a further twenty-five pounds. 'D'you think a little gift would be helpful?'

'Bribe him?'

'They say that every man has his price.'

Jones blew his nose into a large red handkerchief and then energetically prodded around inside each nostril with his forefinger.

.   .   .   .   .

Ryan was at home when the telephone rang on Thursday evening. The caller was Jones.

'I've managed to get that information for you, Mr. Ryan.'

'That's great.'

'It . . . it cost a bit more than you estimated.'

'But then, of course, the job's taken you only two days and not the three I paid you for.'

There was a silence.

'Meet me in Market Square in twenty minutes,' said Ryan. 'That should give you enough time.'

'All right.' The tone of Jones' voice was now sullen. He had judged Ryan an easy touch.

When Ryan replaced the receiver, he turned and for the first time saw Nina had come into the hall.

'Who was that, Hilary?'

He tried to lie. 'A chap from the office.'

'I'm sure it wasn't.' She spoke fiercely. 'What are you up to? For God's sake tell me and don't try to hide things to save me worry. I must know. However bad it is, it's much worse for me when all I can do is guess.'

He looked at her. 'I'm fighting, Nina, fighting with the only weapons I have to try and save our life.'

'What are you talking about? What weapons?'

'Lies, bribery, blackmail.'

She seemed to shiver. 'Things have changed, haven't they?' she murmured, with all the heartbreak yearning of someone who longed to return to the past.

'Yes, they've changed.' He knew he sounded curt, but she had to understand once and for all that they were left without options. Her expression was worried and frightened and yet at the same time proud that he was still fighting for them.

He drove to Market Square and saw Jones' rusting Vauxhall in one of the meter bays. The next but one was empty and he pulled into that. Jones came and sat in the front of the Marina. He handed across a sheet of paper, torn out of a spiral-hinged notebook, on which was written in pencil, in a spidery handwriting, Hal Laurie, sometimes Corney Laurie, last known address twelve, Ibson Lane, Featherston, Birmingham. Five previous convictions, one for dangerous drugs offences.

Jones swept his fingers through his lank black hair. 'It was very tricky going, getting that: very tricky.'

'But you succeeded admirably.'

Jones looked at Ryan, then his shoulders slumped.

'There we are then, Mr. Ryan. If there's anything more I can do for you, just let me know.' He took hold of the door handle.

'As a matter of fact, there is.'

Jones let go of the door handle. 'Just so long as it's perfectly legal.'

Ryan brought out his wallet and counted a hundred and fifty pounds. He folded the notes over and held the wad between forefinger and thumb. Jones stared at the money.

'I want a passport,' said Ryan. 'In the name of George Burton.'

'I can't do that. You've got the wrong man. Just because I've done you a good turn . . .'

Ryan produced a passport photograph, unfolded the money, and put the photograph on the money. He dropped them on Jones' lap. Jones picked them up with jerky movements, as he fought a losing battle against accepting them.

21

Ryan met Jones again on the Saturday evening, in the council car park at the back of the Odeon Cinema. Jones handed across a passport.

'I . . . I shouldn't have done it,' said Jones. His

voice was high and there was an intermittent nervous tic under his right eye. 'I've always been straight before: dead straight. There's been nothing the law could get me on.'

Ryan examined the passport. To his inexpert eyes it was perfect: Foreign Office emboss on the first page and on the photo, particulars page waiting for his entries, issue date a year before and expiry date nine years hence, and on the penultimate page a bank entry to the effect that nine months before he'd drawn a hundred pounds' worth of foreign currency from Barclays Bank in Abston Cross. 'This looks good.'

'It is very good, Mr. Ryan. The man who did it is . . . I'm told he's the acknowledged expert.'

'It's kind of you to have managed the matter so well.'

'That's all right, but I want to make it clear I only did it as a favour—I don't like breaking the law. I've always worked straight.'

Ryan produced an envelope and emptied from it a pile of five-pound notes into his lap.

'I don't know what you're thinking now, Mr. Ryan, but it ain't no good asking me. I'm not doing anything more. That's final.'

Ryan counted aloud. When he smoothed out the last note and added it to the pile, the total was seven hundred and sixty-five. 'There's one last little job I want you to do for me.'

'No!' In his excitement, Jones sprayed the air with saliva. 'I told you: I ain't doing nothing more.'

'I want you to get hold of something belonging to Hal Laurie that has his fingerprints on it.'

168

'Christ! You must be mad!' yelped Jones. He opened the door.

'There's seven hundred and sixty-five pounds for this one small job.'

'I wouldn't touch it if you was offering seven thousand.'

'Why not?'

'Why not?' Jones grew still more excited. 'Because I'm not a thief, that's why not. Because I'm not nicking anything from anybody. . . . And because I'm not getting within miles of a bloke like Laurie.'

'I'm not asking for anything valuable. Just something like a cigarette case, if possible, which has obviously been made in England.'

Jones began to climb out.

'I'm sorry if I've got to tell Detective Superintendent Foxley that you bribed one of his men for information and also supplied me with a forged passport.'

Jones returned to his seat. He slammed the door shut, as if terrified they'd be overheard even though the nearest person was over fifty yards away. 'You can't tell him anything. You're in this as thick as me'

'This is chicken-feed compared to the rest of my troubles.'

Jones lit a cigarette with trembling hands. 'I tell you, I can't,' he whined.

'You've no option, not if you don't want to be arrested—which will finish both you and your job.'

'You . . . you're a bastard.' He looked almost as if about to burst into tears. 'What d'you think Laurie'll do to me?'

'Nothing, if you're careful. He won't know.'

169

'But I . . . I can't nick something of his. I don't know how.

'You've proved yourself resourceful and with useful friends. You'll find a way.'

'I tell you, I can't.'

Ryan passed over the money.

22

The plane circled above the sun-drenched island and for the second time the captain announced over the P.A. system that he was sorry about the delay but that Palma airport was very, very busy that morning.

Ryan stared out of the porthole at the different segments of Majorca that became visible as the aircraft slowly turned to starboard. He studied the mountains, looking quite small and peaceful from a height, and tried to pick out the road from Santa Maria to Orient, but although he identified Soller to give a reference point, he could see no road at all amongst the foothills.

His returning on a forged passport was so great a gamble that he tried, without success, to think of other things. Immigration might pick out the forgery, the Majorcan police might have decided the disappearance of the man was murder and have carried out a search in the pine woods far more extensive than any he had reckoned on, Foxley might not have been fooled and was watching every move. . . .

The captain announced they'd now been given permission to land and the aeroplane came round to head into the sun: a rainbow formed in Ryan's porthole. The signals to stop smoking and fasten seatbelts were switched on and the two stewardesses and the steward walked up and down the ganway to make certain the orders were being obeyed.

The airport was like a place under siege, bursting with people who rushed this way and that: incomprehensible announcements in incomprehensible languages were constantly broadcast.

With such a frantic press of work, Immigration could hardly have been less interested in his passport. The official opened it, closed it, and handed it back, all in one movement. Ryan went through to the luggage area and eventually his single suitcase came through on the conveyor belt. He walked through the seething mass of people in the main hall and out to the taxi rank. Calle de Caro, number forty-seven, he said to the driver: it was a car-hire firm. The driver gestured with both hands and barely missed a bus as he accelerated away. A car-hire firm? His brother-in-law ran the best one in Palma, which meant it was the best in the islands, which meant it was the best in Spain. Other firms were crooked, renting out broken-down SEAT and Simcas with tens of thousands of kilometres unrecorded, no brakes, worn tyres, and burst engines, but his brother-in-law's cars were virtually new.

They drove to a hole-in-the-wall garage, close by the Luis Sitjar stadium, in a road filled with children who dangerously ignored all the traffic. He was shown, with a display of what appeared to be pride, a SEAT that was old, battered, and with tyres worn almost smooth. He agreed to pay one thousand pesetas for the day's hire and he hoped the car would last that long. When asked to sign the hire contract form, with its imaginative English translation, he began to write his own name and had then hurriedly to squiggle that into George Burton. He paid over a thousand-peseta note and the taxi-driver's brother-in-law thanked him profusely, as if this were, indeed, an unusual occasion.

He left Palma and drove through the hot plain, past all the small windmills that made anyone with imagination expect to meet Don Quixote on horse-back, fields of corn and stubble, orchards, vineyards, sprawling clumps of cacti, and herds of sheep and goats. At Santa Maria he turned off on to the Orient road. Immediately, he suffered both a desire to go as quickly as possible to get the whole thing over and done with and an equally strong desire to go as slowly as possible to put it off until the very last moment.

Soon, some of the scenery was familiar: the side of the hill that jutted out, the solitary farmhouse with grey shutters and so few cultivated fields around it that it was almost impossible to imagine how the farmer made a living, Algendar perched on the side of the bare hill with children playing in the rough square. Beyond Algendar, by some quirk of memory, he remembered all the road: the sharp climb out of the village, the right turn, the press of trees, the ruined house perched on the spur of rock, the right-hand bend . . .

He searched for signs of other people and saw none. He drew off the road on to the hard-packed bare ground which formed a natural lay-by and switched off the engine.

He climbed out of the car. The air was heady with the scent of pine, thyme, and lavender. The few deciduous trees rustled in the very light breeze, there was the faint tinkle of a sheep or goat bell, and the everlasting chirping of the cicadas, otherwise peace and quiet.

The sunshine reached down through the trees to warm his face as he patted the pocket of his coat. Inside was a small, metal-covered pad, the kind of thing used for telephone messages or shopping lists, with 'Souvenir of Manchester' stamped on the lid. Jones had handed it to him as if it were liable to explode. It appeared Hal Laurie was an inveterate billiards player at a penny a point in a billiards saloon in Birmingham. He was a careful gambler, keeping a daily record of losses and wins and a running total for the year. Up until June the seventeenth, he'd won a hundred and thirty-four pounds fifty-six pence, which suggested he was a good player. The pages after that date had been carefully torn out by Ryan.

The quiet remained unbroken. He made his way up the slope, all his senses heightened by tension, to the tumbledown well and as he approached he became aware of a stench that would instinctively have made him think of decay even had he not known only too well its cause.

The easiest thing would have been just to throw the pad on top of the bricks which covered the body, but he'd judged that not good enough: the pad must actually be found with the body. He climbed down into the well and here the stench was so concentrated that he gagged. Frantically, he took a handkerchief from his pocket and covered his nose and mouth with it and this did seem to give some relief.

He began to remove the bricks. Underneath was a seething, surging mass of white maggots and the sight of these made him cry out with horror. He threw the pad down into them and then suddenly saw he had one maggot on his right hand, picked up from a brick. Wildly, he brushed it off and sweat tumbled down his face.

He climbed out of the well and staggered across to a tree which he leaned against as he drew deep breaths of clean air into his lungs and tried to think of something, anything, other than that wriggling mass.

There was one last thing which had to be done. Until now, the body had had to remain hidden: now it must be found as soon as possible. After removing the handkerchief from his face, he listened intently until he heard a tinkle to the right. He walked carefully in the direction of the sound and after a while found one sheep on its own, grazing a patch of browned, straggly grass which somehow managed to grow under the closely knit pine trees. He watched and waited and after a time became convinced that the shepherd was not in the immediate vicinity. He moved forward and the sheep watched him without any signs of fear, walking on only at the last minute. He followed easily and in no time the sheep was accepting his presence. Soon, he was able to get very close. He threw himself at the sheep, cracked his nose on its head, hurt his knee on the ground, and was kicked in the thigh. The docile animal seemed to have become a dervish, but he managed to get a firm grip on its fleece and then it abruptly gave up the struggle, merely bleating pathetically. He carried it to the well.

Using old and dirtied string he'd brought with him, he attached one end round the foreleg of the sheep, in such a manner it could have got like that by accident, and the other end round a stout piece of branch. He wedged the branch between the trunks of two closely growing trees. The sheep jerked at its tethered leg for a time, but then resigned itself to this strange state of confinement and began to crop the vegetation within reach. From time to time, its movements made the bell about its neck tinkle.

Ryan returned to the car. The peasant farmers around here, living perpetually close to poverty, would know immediately if one of their sheep was missing. The owner would search for it and when he found it he could not miss the significance of the stench from the well.

23

Detective Superintendent Foxley, dressed in a broadly checked suit that made him look like a robust country squire up from his rolling acres in the Shires, took his pipe from his coat pocket and rubbed the bowl against the palm of his left hand. He looked across Ryan's office desk. 'So the Spanish

Cuerpo General de Policia in Majorca sent us photos, including those of the prints that were found on this metal covered writing pad.'

Ryan fiddled with a pencil. Through the opened window came the harsh crackle of the newly built Formula One Drew with modified side petrol tanks and front spoilers and with an air scoop to the injection trumpets, which was circulating the test track on its initial run.

Foxley filled the pipe with his usual care. 'The prints were identified as those of Hal Laurie, a villain in his late thirties, who's graduated from juvenile vandalism to armed robbery and then to running a dope syndicate that's tied in with the Mafia, or Cosa Nostra, in the States.'

He struck a match and lit his pipe. Clouds of acrid smoke swirled about the room, to be gradually drawn out through the window. 'Laurie admitted the pad was his. The last entry in it was for June the seventeenth.'

'That's the day before I met the runner in Majorca.'

'I thought you'd probably recognise the significance of that date,' said Foxley. He was silent for a while. 'Initially, Laurie denied ever having gone to Majorca, murdering the French runner, forcing you to act as runner, or being in any way still connected with the drug racket.'

'Then how did he explain the pad?'

'He says he lost it and now it's obvious it was stolen from him. The pages torn out dealt with the days after June the seventeenth on which he'd played billiards and the whole thing's an attempted frame-up.

Naturally, we've checked out his alibis and as far as they go they're confirmed.'

'Why as far as they go?' asked Ryan, a trifle hoarsely.

'The men providing his alibi are all villains and all but three are in his mob.'

'What . . . what happens now, then?'

'It's more to the point to ask what did happen. As soon as Laurie was identified from the prints, I was contacted and I went up to the Midlands to work with the local C.I.D. They obtained warrants and searched the homes of him and his known associates. In Laurie's place were fifteen and a half ounces of uncut heroin and seventeen half ounce "pieces" of very heavily cut heroin. If you don't get the significance of those figures, I'll explain. They suggest an original sixteen ounces of uncut heroin, which is the standard weight for international transport by runner, from which half an ounce had been taken. Before transmission to the States, the half-ounce would have been replaced with quinine and the chances would have been all against detection because of the relatively slight degree of adulteration—always presuming the mixing was expertly carried out. . . . Did you know mixing was a highly skilled job, carried out in clinical conditions wearing surgical face-masks? . . . The stolen half-ounce had been mixed with quinine and the seventeen half-ounce pieces, at an even greater degree of adulteration than the normal one to ten, were to be sold to poor devils of addicts in this country. . . . There is no honour at all between thieves, Mr. Ryan. The only question is, what can one get away with without being uncovered?'

177

Ryan uncomfortably wondered if there was special significance in those words.

'The heroin and quinine were analysed. The heroin had almost certainly been manufactured in the South of France. The quinine powder had a very slight impurity that was in the order of point nought five but sufficient to identify it with a laboratory in West Manchester. The quinine was followed through and one lot was traced by a slice of luck to a man called Yardley who's known to be in Laurie's mob.'

'Yardley's an old lag with a string of convictions and a further conviction for drugs must be severe. So he decided to sing like a contralto in the hopes the police will tell the court how helpful he's been and the court won't chuck the book at him.' Foxley's tone was contemptuous.

'Did his evidence help?' asked Ryan. It was impossible yet to judge from Foxley's manner what the outcome of this meeting was going to be.

'It implicated Laurie and detailed much of his organisation, gave a good lead for the French police to work on, and said very little about the set-up in the States. It detailed how the runners in this country were enrolled. Of course, we already knew that part of it.'

Ryan lit a cigarette.

'By the way, you may care to find some consolation in the fact that according to Yardley only a very few of the men approached ever turned the job down after the first dummy run.'

Ryan was uncomfortably aware of the renewed contempt in Foxley's voice.

Foxley puffed at his pipe. 'It was an ingenious

178

scheme. Any runner could be ditched by them or picked up by us at any time without the slightest risk of betrayal.'

'Because he couldn't know a thing,' said Ryan quickly.

'Quite so.'

'And if he couldn't know, then he . . .' Ryan stopped.

'You were going to say?'

'I . . . I've forgotten.'

'Would it have been the proposition that since you couldn't possibly know Laurie was bossing the syndicate, you couldn't steal something belonging to him to plant on the dead runner, Matisse, in Majorca?'

'I wasn't going to say anything like that,' muttered Ryan.

'Because that's what Laurie claimed the moment he was forced to accept the fact that we'd got him nailed on the drugs charges and that you'd been working with us. Matisse must somehow have recognised you were double-crossing the mob and therefore either you killed him to silence him or he tried to kill you but you got in first.'

'But that's absurd.'

'Is it?'

'They gave me that final dummy run from Majorca. . . .'

'Laurie says you brought in heroin: the heroin found in his house.'

'You know that's a lie for a start. The package I handed you contained quinine.'

'That's fact.'

179

'Then if a switch was made, only the dead man, Matisse, could have made it.'

'Certainly, if there was one, it was made in Majorca. Further, if Matisse made the switch intending to steal the heroin from the mob but Laurie already suspected his double-cross, then there's a motive against Laurie.'

'And Laurie's allegation that I brought in heroin is merely an attempt to fix me.'

'That must follow.'

'Then what . . . ?' Ryan stopped.

Foxley drew on his pipe, but it had gone out. 'Matisse's death is a matter for the Majorcan police, but naturally Laurie's statements have been checked and it is fact that there's no record of his having gone out to Majorca. On the other hand, we did find that on one of the flights out on the day of the night that Matisse's body was discovered a George Burton, whose address in England proved to be false, made the return journey.'

'Then you think . . . ?'

'It's impossible to say whether there's any connexion. No one can remember anything about Burton and we've nothing to suggest his quick flight had anything to do with Matisse.'

'So do you believe any of Laurie's absurd accusations about me?'

Foxley put his pipe in his pocket. 'For there to be any truth in them, there's one essential requirement —you must have stolen that pad from him. And how would a man of your background successfully steal anything from a man of his?'

'It's impossible.'

Foxley stood up. 'I suppose "Improbable" would

180

be a better word.' He stared straight at Ryan. 'Never ever forget one thing—you've been lucky.'

'Lucky?'

'Because the sixteen ounces of heroin hadn't been moved on.'

'I don't see . . .'

'You should do.' Foxley's voice sharpened: his expression suddenly held a hint of cruelty. 'I once told you a little about how I feel over drugs and the people who handle them. You got mixed up in the stinking business just to try and save your privileged way of life.'

'I didn't know . . .'

'You chose not to know, and in my book that's the same thing.' Foxley rubbed his chin. His voice calmed. 'But I can be certain you didn't handle dope until the Majorcan trip and then if you did you were lucky because it never got distributed. If it had been, Mr. Ryan, I'd've checked you inside out.'

Ryan spoke very quickly. 'When you're fighting . . .' He stopped.

'You're again lucky. I respect a fighter.' Foxley walked over to the door. Hand on the handle, he said: 'You've been forced to learn a few things about yourself. Don't be in too much of a hurry to let yourself forget them.' He left, slamming the door shut behind him.

Ryan lit a cigarette. There were many of his friends whom he didn't give a damn what they thought about him: yet he wanted Foxley, who could perhaps fancifully be called one of his enemies, to like and respect him and was bitterly saddened because this was impossible. Did he vainly seek such relationship because Foxley was the man he himself

181

had once been, loyal to justice?, and had Foxley, despite all his quiet intelligence, never allowed himself to appreciate the fact that ideals could sometimes be luxuries? . . .

.   .   .   .   .

Anderson scooped up the cards. 'It's my deal now, but we'll pause long enough to wet our whistles.'

When they played poker at his flat, he offered an embarrassingly constant succession of drinks of great variety, as if he felt an overwhelming need to prove the boundless extent of his hospitality.

'Polly, my love, what's yours?' he asked.

'No more for me, thanks,' she answered, 'or you'll see me on all fours.'

'Go on and give us the chance.'

She chuckled as she shook her head.

'Nina, then, what about you?'

'I'm fine at the moment.'

'Hell, what is this? A teetotaller's convention in mourning? Pete, you're not training on water, I know.'

'I will have just a drop of Scotch, then, Ted.'

'Hilary—are you ready to live dangerously?'

'Give me another Cinzano and just step clear.'

Anderson took Comyns' and Ryan's glasses across to the cocktail cabinet and refilled them. As he handed Ryan's glass back, he said: 'How's the new job going?'

'Quite well. It's a lot more interesting than at Llanarchs and management's attitude to methods of work is totally different.'

'And you haven't landed in any problems with them over all this smuggling?'

'On the contrary. Because I was helping the police right from the beginning, all the publicity tends to create a good image for Drew, whose name keeps cropping up. Before you know where you are, they'll be promoting me to the board.'

Anderson gave himself another drink and returned to his chair. 'That's just great! Any time I can be of help, Hilary, just give the word. I know one or two people who can be useful and who owe me a good turn.'

'That's really most kind and generous of you,' replied Ryan, with a sarcasm heavy enough to bring a warning frown to Nina's face.

'Always like to give a friend a leg up. Now then, everyone, let's get the pasteboards swirling, the money whirling. I warn you all, here and now, I'm feeling real lucky.' He dealt the cards.

Ryan bought two, Nina threw in, Comyns bought one, Polly two and Anderson three.

Ryan opened with a white chip. Comyns matched, Polly threw in, and Anderson raised a white chip.

'Let's make it a bit more expensive,' said Ryan. 'Up twenty.' He added a green chip.

'You've moved out of my class.' Comyns threw in.

Anderson stared sideways at Ryan and then at the chips in front of him. 'You keep hitting hard to-night.'

'Why blame me if I get good cards.'

Anderson looked disgruntled. 'Raise you five.'

'Don't be too rash.' Ryan added two green chips. 'There's another forty to make you palpitate.'

Anderson nibbled his lower lip. He swore as he threw in. 'My two pairs aren't much good when you've got threes at the very least.'

Ryan smiled as collected his winnings.

'You did have threes, didn't you?' demanded Anderson.

Ryan's smile broadened. He flipped over his hand to show a pair of fours.

'What the hell's got into you?' said Anderson, unable to hide his annoyance at being beaten by a bluff.

'Maybe I've at last learned how to gamble successfully,' Ryan replied.